AN OLD-FASHIONED PRACTICE

District Nurse Daisy Rose could tell that Josh Cameron would be a new broom, when he came to run the practice while his father, Theo, recovered from a heart attack. Despite feeling instant attraction to Josh, Daisy felt torn by her loyalty to Theo, who preferred old-fashioned methods. Besides, Josh had made it clear he would be moving on when Theo came back, so Daisy would be a fool to become intimately involved with him – and had to accept that she was just such a fool, in love...

AN OLD-FASHIONED PRACTICE

An Old-Fashioned Practice

by

Carol Wood

Dales Large Print Books
Long Preston, North Yorkshire,
BD23 4ND, England.

British Library Cataloguing in Publication Data.

Wood, Carol
    An old-fashioned practice.

    A catalogue record of this book is
    available from the British Library

    ISBN   978-1-84262-516-3 pbk

First published in Great Britain in 1996 by
Mills & Boon Limited

Copyright © Carol Wood 1996

Cover illustration © Ben Turner by arrangement with
P.W.A. International Ltd.

The moral right of the author has been asserted

Published in Large Print 2007 by arrangement with
Dorian Literary Agency

Dales Large Print is an imprint of Library Magna Books Ltd.

Printed and bound in Great Britain by
T.J. (International) Ltd., Cornwall, PL28 8RW

CHAPTER ONE

Daisy had always turned heads.

It was a perfectly understandable reaction from people who, having never set eyes on her before, were compelled to look twice at the startling cloud of ebony hair encircling sea-green eyes set deeply in a heart-shaped face.

It was not surprising, therefore, when Daisy strolled into Dr Cameron's waiting room on a hot July morning, that she turned a number of heads, one after the other, as she passed by.

'Kathleen!' Daisy exclaimed in surprise, recognising one of the doctor's patients, an elderly lady who was normally housebound. 'How did you manage to travel into surgery–?'

Before Daisy could finish asking her question a loud crash from Dr Theo Cameron's room brought the soft murmur of voices in the waiting room to an abrupt halt. The next thing Daisy saw was Emily Fields, the practice secretary, stumbling from the consulting room, her notebook tumbling from her hands as she steadied herself against the reception desk. 'D-Daisy ... quickly ... it's

Dr Cameron! I think it's his heart!'

For a second, Daisy didn't move. Emily must be mistaken, she thought as her mind whirled frantically, searching for a logical explanation. Though Dr Theo had been unwell for some time he'd had his check-up only last week; his medication had been updated … he'd even said he'd begun to feel better…

But then, staring at Emily's stricken face, Daisy forced herself into action, her long legs seeming to move too slowly as she ran into the doctor's room, almost falling over the old mahogany desk in her hurry to get round it.

Theodore Cameron lay sprawled on the ancient oriental carpet that had been installed more than thirty years previously, his face grey, his old tweed jacket, always buttoned even in summer, wrenched open across his chest.

She sank to her knees. Swiftly searching for a pulse, her fingers went first to his neck and then to his wrist.

Nothing at all. Not even a flicker.

Vaguely she heard the sounds of the outside world – Emily stammering into the phone calling the emergency services, the reverberation of traffic on the busy road, hushed murmurs of agitation from the waiting room…

Still no pulse.

Skin colour grey. Lips blue.

Daisy steadied her position above the unconscious man and stiffened her back, preparing herself for the sharp, decisive thump she must give with a clenched fist to the left lower half of the doctor's breastbone.

She gave it. She checked again. No response.

For the first time ever in her nursing career fear paralysed her. You're too late, a little voice whispered inside her; you've lost him.

Daisy shut out the voice, forcing herself to concentrate on the set of compressions she must make; rocking forwards, heel of one hand on the lower third of the breastbone, heel of the other covering it ... arms straight, push down smoothly and firmly...

After the fifth compression she bent to give a single breath by mouth-to-mouth. Tiny beads of perspiration sprinkled her brow, dampness ran down her spine under her summer dress, causing the cloth to cling to her limply. She paused, her own heart thudding, deafening her as she thought of precious seconds ticking by and still no response.

'It's all right, I've a pulse,' said a deep voice beside her. 'Faint, but it's there. Keep going.'

She turned her head briefly to find a man crouching beside her. A man with deep grey eyes. 'A pulse?' she repeated. 'Are you sure?'

As though to prove his point, the stranger's

11

fingers guided her own over a limp and fragile wrist until Daisy felt the blessed flicker of life for herself.

'Keep going, or do you want me to take over?' The grey eyes were filled with deep concern, belying the hard edge to his voice.

She shook her head, pausing only briefly to wonder who he was, before she bent down to continue the respiration.

It was much later, when the ambulance had gone and Daisy and Emily had managed to clear the waiting room of patients, attending to all those they could help in Dr Theo's absence, that Daisy recalled the strong hands of the stranger moving around her waist and gently lifting her from beside Dr Theo to guide her to sit on the worn leather consulting chair.

'Will you be all right,?' he'd asked eventually as he'd handed over Dr Theo to the paramedics. 'I'll go with my father if you can cope here.'

Daisy remembered nodding until suddenly she'd realised what he'd said. 'Your ... father?'

'Josh ... Josh Cameron.' He'd given her a brief smile. 'Will you be OK?'

She'd nodded again. 'Yes, yes, of course. Er ... if you can let us know...?'

'As soon as I can.'

Then, as though in a trance, she had

watched him follow the stretcher out, tall and broad-shouldered, a man with incredibly deep grey eyes, leaving behind him a subtle scent which had made her swallow as she'd breathed it in.

Now, several hours later, as she sat with Emily in the small treatment room drinking a hot cup of tea, liberally sugared, Daisy tried to piece together the mysterious appearance of the man she had previously formed a mental picture of, but had never seen in the flesh until today.

Somehow the two didn't quite fit together. Helen and Theo hadn't often talked about him, but when they did she had managed to glean that their son was quite a celebrity in the world of medical research. Funny, she always thought of researchers as bespectacled professors in rumpled old suits. This man looked more like a...

Now what was it? An actor, yes. He had unusually tanned skin – and not from a sunbed – a slow, deep, very English voice, casual, confident grace as he moved...

'I can't believe it,' Emily sighed, interrupting Daisy's thoughts as she slumped in a chair, nervously tucking her dishevelled brown bun back into its knot. 'One minute Dr Theo was talking to me quite normally, the next–' Without warning she burst into tears.

Daisy recognised the reaction as delayed

shock and, lowering her cup to the desk, went over to slide an arm around the narrow, shaking shoulders. 'Emily, Dr Theo's alive,' she whispered gently. 'He stands every chance of recovery. Come on, this isn't like you! Let's look on the positive side.'

The secretary blinked tearfully up at Daisy's face, a lovely, fine-featured face shrouded by dark waves which fell across her shoulders and spilled over the rose print dress.

'He's going to be just fine.' Daisy spoke cheerfully despite her doubts. Dear, reliable little spinster Emily who had worked so hard to help Dr Cameron over the last two exceptionally difficult years. Not only had she borne the brunt of the doctor's frustration after his car crash, but she had a heart of gold for all the patients too.

Just then a voice rang out from somewhere in the building and Emily jerked up her head. 'Reception! Goodness, we didn't lock the outer doors, did we?'

Daisy gave a sigh. 'Probably just someone for a prescription. Better make sure, though.'

Both women made their way along the hall. When they reached the waiting room, Daisy's green eyes opened wide. She couldn't tell by Josh Cameron's face whether it was bad news – not until he walked closer, and by that time her heart was almost lifting out of her chest.

'It's all right,' he told them calmly. 'He's stable. He's out of danger.'

Daisy and Emily let out a combined sigh and for a brief second Daisy found it impossible to speak. 'Is he ... fully conscious?' she asked, biting back the emotion in her voice.

'Yes, he's in the cardiac care unit and asking to see you.' He looked at her uncertainly. 'Sister Rose, isn't it?'

'He remembers what happened?' she gasped in surprise.

'Just fragments. Enough to want to thank you for what you did for him.' A flash of white teeth appeared under the deep tan and Daisy realised she was looking into the most unusual eyes she had ever seen in her life. She had thought them a beautiful silvery grey before, but now she wasn't certain. Now they were a kind of smoky blue ... or perhaps, disarmingly, a bit of both.

He also had a headily expensive taste in dress, unlike Dr Theo and his beloved but ancient cords and tweeds which saw him through summer and winter alike. Dressed in tailored sand-coloured clothes, polished brown shoes, and with hair as thick and dark as her own, Theo's son bore not the faintest resemblance to his father.

'And it's Emily, isn't it? Didn't we meet briefly once a couple of years back?'

'Yes...' Emily blushed furiously. 'Just after

15

the accident.'

'Ah ... yes.' His face darkened and he seemed briefly lost in thought, bringing up a large hand to run it through the thick, black, perfectly groomed hair.

The sudden silence caused Daisy to remember the few details Emily had passed on to her about Theo Cameron's car accident and how as a result Helen, his wife, had lost the use of her legs.

Daisy realised she was just beginning to think straight again and a great deal was falling into place, not much of which, regarding the doctor's son, she liked.

Ungluing her eyes from the mesmeric stare, she did a rapid double take. The Camerons' son was a doctor with a burgeoning career in specialist research. But the fact remained that he had also been conspicuously absent from the upheavals in his parents' lives over the past few years, except for that one flying visit shortly after the accident which Emily had told her about. OK, so he had worked in America and Australia – either way, the air service from both continents was pretty regular!

And what of helping to resolve the ensuing problems of a one-man practice like his father's? He must have known how Theo had struggled.

What had finally brought him halfway across the world to see Helen and Theo? she

16

wondered curiously. What kind of selfish nature lay beneath the sensual curve of mouth set under the high, carved brown cheek bones?

Josh Cameron gave her a curious look. 'You're wondering why I'm here?' he paused for a moment, the grey eyes skimming over their faces. 'I arrived from Florida last night – though Theo and Helen didn't know I was coming. I'm on my way to a multinational medical conference in Sydney–'

'Oh, I'm sure Dr Theo and Helen were delighted to see you ... er, even under these – um – circumstances,' Emily interrupted, completely overawed.

He smiled. 'Thank you, Emily.' He turned slowly to Daisy. 'Will you come to the hospital to see Theo?'

Her mind grappled with the strangeness of hearing him call his parents by their Christian names. She couldn't imagine calling her own parents anything but Mum and Dad, treasured words which even now, fifteen years after their deaths, she still missed using.

Still, it took all types, she decided philosophically and tried hard to give the man in front of her the benefit of the doubt. Even so, poor Helen. As if the accident and the spinal injury that had committed her to a wheelchair hadn't been enough, now there was this trauma to contend with.

'You aren't on your rounds, are you?' he

asked as she moved away to find her things.

'It's my day off today but as it was a fine morning I walked to the practice to clarify one or two messages I'd left for your father and then – well, you know the rest.'

'In that case I'll drive you.'

'No, I can go back home for my–'

'I really don't think there's time.'

Daisy hesitated, then shrugged. She went to collect her bag and sweater from the room that Angela, the practice nurse, used for her natal clinic, aware of Emily talking to the man with the piercing grey eyes, hearing his deep and resonant voice ebb and flow through the surgery.

For the first time she noticed a resemblance to his father. The voice held enormous power – a no-nonsense voice, as her Uncle Toby would have called it.

Her heart gave a little twist as she listened, thinking of Theo. His stubborn and sometimes impossible ways were the ones which she now missed him all the more for even in the short space of time he'd been gone.

Well, for his and Helen's sake she would be cordial to their son, but it was going to be difficult, very difficult, for all she knew of his hard-hearted ways.

Josh Cameron drove a steel-grey Mercedes. 'It's hired,' he told her bluntly as he slid in behind the wheel. 'Just for the short period

18

of time I'm here.'

Point taken, Daisy thought waspishly. 'The short period of time'. In other words, I'm *en route* to my oh, so crucial medical conference and nothing is going to stop me from getting there!

'I have to thank you for what you did for Theo.' She watched his large brown hands turn the steering wheel and nose the car along Summerforde high street. 'You do realise you saved his life?'

She hesitated, studying the long, straight nose, powerful square chin and impeccable ebony-black hair ending in a softly smoothed line just above his collar. 'You were beside me but you didn't stop me. Why?' she asked curiously.

'Why should I? You were doing everything possible for him. I couldn't have done any better.'

If the position had been reversed and it had been her father lying on the floor instead ... well, she was pretty sure she wouldn't have remained so totally in control as Josh Cameron had seemed to be.

They drove in silence to the cottage hospital. He seemed to know the way so she didn't bother to give any directions. When they arrived he politely opened her door, escorted her along the polished white corridors to CCU, and guided her to one of the three hydraulic beds in the ward. It was surrounded by an array of sophisticated equipment. Above it all she caught the ominous blinking of the heart monitor.

The soft, artificial light made Helen Cameron, in her wheelchair, look almost unreal. Careful to avoid the intravenous lines and smiling warmly at Helen, Daisy bent to squeeze Theo's free hand.

He opened rheumy eyes and gave her a wonky little smile. 'Bad luck,' he whispered. 'You're not rid of me yet, my girl.'

She mumbled something in answer, her throat constricting.

Helen Cameron bent forward, her fingers closing gently over Daisy's wrist. 'We shall never be able to thank you enough, Daisy. The doctors think he has a good chance of a full recovery, but only if–' She hesitated, giving a little shrug, and Daisy understood. Her husband had survived, but there was a price to be paid, and knowing the doctor as she did – a man whose life was totally dedicated to his work – Daisy was well aware that it would take all of Helen's ingenuity to keep him away from his patients for any length of time.

'I'll be back,' he muttered predictably, trying to form words through slow-moving lips. 'Tell young Keen not to get too comfortable in my chair.'

Daisy smiled. Dr Keen was the locum doctor who stood in when necessary and would doubtlessly take over this time. 'Just get well,' she whispered, feeling disconnected from her body all of a sudden as Theo closed his eyes.

He drifted back into sleep, and Daisy laid down his hand on the white sheet. She dared not look at Helen, not for the moment. But she was aware of Josh moving towards her, of his touch on her shoulder.

His gesture did seem to help. She pulled herself together quickly and summoned a smile for Helen. 'I'll ring you,' she whispered. 'Let me know if there's anything … anything at all I can do.'

Helen drew her head down and kissed her cheek. It was a while before Daisy steadied herself, swallowing down the enormous lump in her throat. When she looked up, Josh was motioning her to go with him.

'He'll be pretty out of it for a while,' he said softly as they walked together from the ward. 'But it's a good thing. He'll get plenty of rest.'

'He's so stubborn – so determined,' she croaked as the doors closed behind them.

'Which is why he survived.'

'But he needs to slow down – he'll burn himself out otherwise.'

Theo Cameron's son nodded. 'Maybe. But it's his life. He has to live it his way.'

Daisy's green eyes sparkled as the quietness in the corridor loomed around them. 'Your

21

mother might disagree with you. I think she would say she has a vested interest somewhere along the line.'

The point went home and the grey eyes cooled. 'Theo is the man she married. Helen has always known his work comes above and beyond everything else.'

'B-but people compromise,' she found herself spluttering. 'A heart attack is a warning; he has to take notice and start to live–'

'Wrapped in cotton wool?' he suggested cynically.

Daisy narrowed her lovely eyes. 'No, I didn't mean that. I just meant he has to take stock, must take care for your mother's sake–'

'Daisy ... she understands him. It's entirely their business.'

'Meaning?'

He shrugged. 'Look, this isn't getting us very far. I'll drive you home.'

She shook her head. She'd had enough of Josh Cameron for one day. 'No, thanks. I'll make my own way.'

'Don't be ridiculous. If you won't let me drive you, at least let me get you a taxi.'

She moved away. 'I'd rather walk. It's not far.'

He raised a wry eyebrow. 'Are you always so stubborn?'

'It depends...'

His chuckle was self-deprecating. 'On the

22

company you're in, I suppose?'

The attractive grin was enough to rattle her composure and she found herself smiling too, despite the fact that he'd had the nerve to tell her, very firmly, very politely, to mind her own business.

'Better let you go, then,' he sighed.

She hesitated. 'You'll let me know if there is any news?'

He nodded. 'I'll let you know.'

She turned, hurrying down the corridor, feeling the skin in the middle of her shoulders prickle.

Outside in the fresh air, she stood still and closed her eyes. Josh Cameron's message had come across loud and clear. Leave Theo and Helen alone. It was as plain as day. Irrespective of how close she was to the doctor and his wife, their son had just firmly warned her off from becoming involved in his parents' affairs.

Daisy gazed at her cornflakes without appetite. Her pride was still hurting. Badly.

All she had been doing was offering her modest opinion. And he had firmly returned it to her – despite the fact that he hadn't seen his parents for goodness knew how long.

Uncle Toby harpooned the silver backing of the pill pack with a knife. 'These will be the end of me,' he complained morosely.

Daisy watched him ladle strawberry jam

over his buttered toast. 'It won't be your medication that'll be your end, Uncle Toby – more like jam poisoning.' But he wasn't listening, as usual, turning a perfectly healthy deaf ear her way.

She sighed, glancing back to the mirror as she tightened her black belt around her slim waist, smoothing her dark blue uniform into place. Her uncle's ulcer was a bone of contention between them.

Deciding this was definitely not the morning to argue, Daisy decided to phone the hospital and find out how Theo was. The CCU sister was helpful and actually intimated that he was improving.

Having put the phone down, much cheered, she bent to kiss her uncle on the cheek. 'See you for your lunch?'

'Don't trouble yourself for me. I'll make myself a healthy snack.'

'In the form of your pipe and a cream bun?' Daisy threw over her shoulder and, receiving no answer, smiled to herself as she left the house.

The trouble was that staying at home to boss him about, as he called it, was a mistake she had made two years ago when she had returned home from Paris. Uncle Toby had other ideas. His life at sea hadn't made him a free spirit for nothing, he frequently reminded her.

Her departure from the Marie Claire

clinic on the banks of the Seine where she had worked since qualifying had brought with it mixed emotions, she reflected as she climbed into her chic little red car. She had been sorry to leave the friends she had made, but she had achieved her aim to live and work in the city of her mother's birth.

Daisy spoke good French, taught to her by her mother, Desiree, after whom she was named. Her parents had been a singing duo in the sixties and had toured the world, their base being the family home in Summerforde. But when she was ten her mother had developed an inoperable cancer. Her death had been a blow from which Daisy had barely recovered before her father had died a year later – some said, including Uncle Toby, of a broken heart.

Uncle Toby, her father's brother, had come to her rescue. He'd taken early retirement from the sea to care for her and badger her into her first year of training after her A levels. The badgering had continued until her finals, to the extent that he hadn't even shown the slightest remorse when she'd had the offer to go to Paris.

'Just don't go falling in love with the first Casanova you meet!' he'd warned her before she'd left for the élite Paris clinic.

'The chance would be a fine thing,' she'd joked back, painfully aware that through her adolescence she'd been too busy to become involved in the kind of relationships her friends had experienced. For a start, none of them had an Uncle Toby to contend with! Taking the role of both parents, he wanted the best for her, she knew. But the one time she'd brought a boy home the extent of the interrogation had not boded well for return visits.

Hence she'd kept her friendships at a distance and she'd studied hard.

Once she'd thought she'd been in love. Ned Asher had been a medical student in her year. They'd spent a whole summer together and by Christmas, he'd been putting pressure on her to deepen their relationship.

He was a nice guy. She'd really liked him. And she had been on the point of committing herself when she'd discovered that she wasn't the only one smitten by teasing blue eyes and long, rakish blond hair. Julia Forester, a year below, had had a vested interest as well. It had hurt for a while when she'd found out they were sleeping together.

'You'll have plenty of chances,' Uncle Toby had clumsily comforted her during her blue moods. 'Whoever it is you're mooning over, there'll be another one to fill his shoes. Concentrate on your finals first.'

Perhaps it had been then that she'd decided he was right. Ned Asher had had his hair cut anyway and hadn't looked half as sexy. She'd sunk her pride, immersed herself in her studies and flown through her finals.

And then had come her reward; Paris.

Had she expected to find love there? she wondered now. But she'd been too busy discovering the city with her small circle of friends to stop for breath. Several doctors had taken her out; she liked Frenchmen – they were charming and gracious – and one in particular, Dr Pierre Ruegg, had begun to date her on a regular basis. He was good-looking and fun but she hadn't been in love, just enjoying the idea that she might be.

And when news had reached her of her uncle's illness she'd flown home for good just before her twenty-fourth birthday.

Coming back to the present, Daisy turned her little car into Summerforde high street. On a day like this two years ago she had frog-marched Uncle Toby into the Camerons' surgery.

'Call this a doctor's?' he'd grumbled, glaring around the shabby old Victorian building. 'More like the British Museum!'

'Just sit still and stop complaining while I give in your details,' she had commanded as he'd tipped his sea-cap over his eyes and made himself unavailable to the world.

Even in her wheelchair Helen Cameron had ably manned Reception in the absence of the holidaying secretary, Emily Fields.

Smiling at the memories, Daisy parked

and locked her car, reflecting how lucky she was to have secured the vacancy on the Summerforde DN team. In the main, she had Theo and Helen to thank for it. The fact that she had worked at the Marie Claire had helped, but Dr Theo's recommendation to the local authority had been the deciding factor.

'Morning, Emily!' Daisy tossed back her black hair, a riot of shining waves. 'Has Dr Keen arrived?'

Emily looked past the early-morning patient. 'I'll be with you in a second or two Daisy, hold on–'

But Daisy was already on her way down the narrow hall, eager to greet the locum doctor. Dr Keen was a wee bit abrupt, it was true, but he was always prepared to step in for Dr Theo.

She gazed into the office expectantly. 'Good morn–' She froze.

Josh Cameron stared back at her with those grey, grey eyes.

She stared at the dog-eared pile of records he was holding and her heart sank.

'Dr Keen had an accident on the ski slopes. Nothing too serious – a leg in plaster. So … here I am.'

'B-but your conference … your research…'

He laughed. 'You know, Daisy, you'd make a damn fine PA. I think you've missed your vocation somewhere along the line.'

She watched open-mouthed as he walked past her with the tattered files in his arms. His dark suit and crisp white shirt and snappy tie made him look like a jet-setting executive about to put the final touches to a million-dollar deal.

'Coming?' he called.

Oh, no, let it be a mistake, she prayed as the tall figure moved authoritatively down the hall.

Straightening herself to her full five feet nine – a height advantage she now blessed, for a change – she followed.

'Take a seat.' He gestured to the patient's chair.

She sat.

With a strange fascination she watched him. Precise, orderly, shifting his father's things around on the desk. A sensual flicker of strong white teeth flashed through his lips as he looked up.

'Cards on the table. You don't like me much, Daisy; that's plain enough.'

She started to protest, but he raised his hand to stop her. 'Let's at least try to be honest and get off to a better start than we did yesterday.'

At a loss for words, because he was absolutely right, she nodded.

'Good.' He perched a muscled thigh on the edge of the desk. 'Neither you nor I really have a choice at the moment – unless, of course, you ask for a transfer from the practice.'

She jumped to her feet. 'But I don't want a transfer–'

'Excellent! Apparently you're very good at your job. Theo wouldn't like to lose you. Now sit down, Daisy, and listen – please.'

She sat, slowly, reluctantly, fuming inside. It was, she realised, going to be a long day.

CHAPTER TWO

Daisy continued watching as Josh eased himself comfortably into his father's chair. 'I'm arranging to take a three-month sabbatical from my research in Florida,' he told her carefully.

'Three months?'

'It suits me well enough. I was planning a break after Sydney anyway.'

She felt a cold hand run down her spine. 'And if three months isn't long enough, if his recovery doesn't fit in with your timetable?'

'I don't care to look at the situation negatively.'

'Or realistically?'

He gave her an unamused smile. 'Oh, I'm a realist, Daisy. I wouldn't be working in research if I wasn't. Now, let's get down to work.' He spread the records out in front of him, peeling an ancient strip of tape off one of them. 'These records are falling to pieces. Quite frankly, the paperwork is in chaos.' He looked up at her. 'You seem pretty close to Theo. Have you never discussed this with him?'

Daisy tried to ignore his tone. 'Organised

chaos, your father says,' she told him truthfully. 'He and Emily seem to manage between them.'

The grey eyes came sharply up at her. 'Organised for Theo, maybe, but for no one else. Details should be entered on a computer, then with just a flick of a few keys a patient's medical history can be seen at a glance. They should not be kept in one man's mind, no matter how conscientious he might be.'

'Your father hates machines,' Daisy answered stiffly. 'He blames technology for distancing the doctor from his patient. He believes in the old-fashioned–'

'I know exactly what Theo believes, though you may seriously doubt it.'

She did doubt it, absolutely. He hadn't seen his father for over two years and if he truly appreciated Theo's disdain for computers he certainly wouldn't be making this kind of suggestion.

'Anyway, let's get down to the matter in hand.' He sat back in his father's chair and stared at her. 'This is what I intend to do. For the rest of the week I'm going to concentrate on surgeries, establish myself with as many patients as I can. Then, next week, I should like to meet some of our housebound patients, those on your caseload who you feel are representative as a whole.'

'You mean … you want to come with me

on domiciliary visits?' she asked in astonishment.

'Any objections?'

There were, hundreds. 'Well–' she fumbled, and was promptly interrupted.

'Meeting people in their own surroundings will be an efficient induction back into general practice. Research work is very static, even isolated, so you'll have to bear with me a good deal of the time.'

At least he had the grace to admit it. 'I have another practice I cover too,' she explained hesitantly. 'Four doctors at the Summerforde health centre.' Her conscience made her add. 'Three other nurses cover most of their patients. I have one or two diabetics...'

'No problem. I'll fit in with your schedule.' Something in the grey eyes softened. When they had that expression in them they were beautiful eyes, she decided reluctantly. Fringed with very black, thick lashes. They had lost their cold sea-grey and she couldn't help responding to the energy and enthusiasm expressed in them.

She nodded. 'If that's what you want.'

'Good.' He stood up and she realised that the interview was at a close. Still fascinated by the sensual lilt of the mouth, the glimmering grey eyes under their moist hoods and the dark, grainy skin of his face, she stood up too and was promptly lost for words.

An occurrence Uncle Toby would have greatly appreciated, Daisy reflected wryly, had he been the recipient.

It was a surprising week.

Angela Duffey, the part-time practice nurse, gave in her notice. She had been struggling with a housebound father-in-law, two adolescent children and an asthmatic husband. Finally, after a frightening attack, her husband had been admitted to hospital and transferred to a specialist unit near London. Angela had regretfully decided that for the time being she had too much to cope with to continue her part-time nursing.

'Do you think we can manage until we know if she's coming back?' Josh asked Daisy just before surgery one morning. 'I'll treat her regular patients at the end of surgery but I'm concerned about the natal clinics – they're pretty well patronised at the moment. Everyone seems to be having babies.'

'I'll share them with you if you like,' Daisy offered. 'Do the BP and weights and notes?'

He looked relieved and she wondered if he'd been counting on her to help out. 'Done,' he said with a grin.

'How are you coping?' she asked cautiously, reflecting that during the week she had seen him up to his ears in paperwork and had heard some of the patients giving him a thorough grilling regarding Theo.

He gave her a crooked grin. 'Bob Gordunston over the other side of town, whom Theo used for on-call rota, has been very helpful. He's willing to continue in the same way with me. The patients are straightforward enough but the paperwork is driving me crazy. I don't like working in a mess. Research training, I suppose. I like everything pigeon-holed.'

She wondered if that meant people too. 'Your father seemed to know where to find things.' She made the excuse half-heartedly, for privately she had often worried that the older doctor was becoming inundated with paperwork, and lately if it hadn't been for Emily, he would have been lost.

'Well, let's not get onto that subject.' He shrugged. 'Don't forget next week, after surgery, you're taking me on your rounds.'

She nodded, a curl of attraction flaring inside her as she felt the enthusiasm he generated. Like it or not, he was a motivator. Even the patients seemed to sit up and pull back their shoulders when his voice boomed around the waiting room.

She'd noticed the women, like Emily, shyly letting their gaze rove over his elegant dark suits and reciprocating the smile which broadened quite naturally when he shook their hands and said, 'Hi!' – as he always made a point of doing. A borrowed Americanism, she decided, despite his English breeding. A warm welcome was good psychology for a doctor, more so from a man who was, she imagined, normally immersed in test-tubes.

The following Monday morning, to her surprise, she felt excited at the prospect of working with Josh. When she arrived at the surgery Emily gave her the few messages from the nurse's book.

'Big day today?' Emily gave her a wry smile.

Daisy laughed. 'Heaven knows why, but I feel quite nervous.'

'I know why if heaven doesn't,' Emily grinned.

Daisy blushed. Why on earth was she blushing? 'Oh, I just mean–'

'Only teasing.' Emily chuckled as she unclipped the case from her ancient electric typewriter. 'Most of our patients – the female ones at any rate – all but faint when they see who it is.'

Emily looked up at Daisy and they both burst into laughter. Then they heard the first few patients coming in and Emily put on her glasses, smoothed back her hair – which Daisy noticed she had cut and styled recently – and gave a wink to Daisy as she left for her rounds.

Her morning went smoothly. Two diabetics, a post-op check on a toenail removal and several leg ulcers. Daisy had reserved her most relevant cases for the afternoon and for Josh. She tucked her notes into her case and walked into the surgery at one-thirty, finding Emily at lunch and Josh waiting for her in his father's consulting room.

'Right, where are we off to?' he asked and stood up, gathering his case.

She looked down at her notes. 'I thought Mr Adams and his wife first. Then–'

'And who is Mr Adams?'

She found herself following him through the surgery. 'He had a cerebrovascular accident last year–'

'Local man?' He opened the front door for her and she slipped through.

'Very much so.' She tried to stop thinking how those grey-blue eyes seemed to change colour every time she looked into them – especially now, in the warm sunshine. 'Er, Mr Adams is eighty-two and his wife a few years younger. She has quite a bit on with all the caring and I'm equally concerned for her. She's becoming increasingly limited by arthritis and her BP is high.'

'Fine. I'll come in your car as doubtless you prefer to drive?'

'Oh … right. Yes.' She blinked, surprised at the offer, as he slipped a hand under her elbow and propelled her across the busy road.

As she drove, very conscious of his large body squeezed into the passenger seat beside her, she wondered how he was going to react to the Adamses' house, which was one of the most dilapidated buildings in the neighbourhood.

'Who did you see this morning?' He stretched his long legs and collided with the dashboard.

Looking at them, Daisy stalled the engine. Luckily they were at amber lights and she started the car again, realising how nervous she was. She made yet another effort to concentrate and told him about her morning calls.

He nodded thoughtfully. 'After the Adamses – who else?'

'Two. A young paraplegic woman and a middle-aged lady who has a terminal illness.'

'So ... at least six calls in a day, often more?'

Daisy steered the car slowly into the kerb in front of the Adamses' house. 'Yes, six to ten, depending on the amount of time I spend at each. If I make a drink or a snack for someone if it's required it could delay me and I might have to leave a non-urgent call until the next day.'

Black eyebrows shot up. 'Preparing meals are included in a district nurse's workload?'

'No ... but what else do I do if I find someone who hasn't eaten or drunk properly for several days?'

'Isn't there a food-delivery service?'

'There is, but it takes time and patience to organise. Meanwhile my patient might lapse into a diabetic coma or faint with malnutrition. Am I supposed to let that happen?'

'OK!' He threw her a teasing grin. 'Just checking. Don't forget I'm new around here … you'll have to make allowances for me.'

The way he had for her with his parents? she thought but didn't say.

Still, she wouldn't dwell on it – all water under the bridge. Fair dues, he seemed to be trying now.

Mrs Adams seemed to take an eternity to answer the door after their knock. 'A bad day for my arthritis,' she explained as she showed them into a cluttered and dismal-looking room that had a thick, mildewy odour hanging in the air.

''Scuse the state of the place,' she apologised. 'Damp's getting in a bit here and there.' And Daisy was uncomfortably aware of Josh's gaze running over the stained wallpaper.

She went about her business, however, and changed Mr Adams's catheter bag, attending to his leg with Sudocrem where he had a nasty red sore. 'Thank you, Daisy,' he said with a tiny slur to his speech – a result of his stroke. His gaze went to the doctor who was listening carefully to his wheezy chest through the stethoscope. 'Doctor, would you like a cup of tea?'

39

Mrs Adams called from the kitchen, 'I've just made one,' as Josh Cameron removed the stethoscope from his ears.

'Indeed I would,' he called back, surprising Daisy with his friendliness. And, surprising her even more, he spent another fifteen minutes over tea discussing the problem of the flare-up of Mrs Adams's arthritis, finally making out a prescription for a change from Brufen to another non-steroidal anti-inflammatory drug.

'They are a very independent couple,' Daisy said defensively before her companion uttered a word as they climbed back into the car. 'Despite Mrs Adams's arthritis she refuses to have a home help or meals-on-wheels because – and she's told me this – she feels that the day that happens someone in authority will say she can't cope. She fears being separated from her husband. In fact, the last time he went into hospital she virtually camped at his bedside–'

He held up both hands. 'Hey, slow down. You don't have to defend them to me.'

She stiffened. 'I wasn't. I was just–'

'You were. And I'm impressed. I can see your heart's in the right place, Daisy, but I'm wondering...' He gave her an uncertain look. 'With no downstairs bathroom it must be extremely frustrating, especially in winter. Have they never thought of having the house modernised?'

She eyed him warily. 'Modernised? But that would cost a lot of money. Isn't it obvious that they aren't in a position to afford such luxuries?'

He shrugged. 'Surely there is alternative accommodation? Could they be put on a waiting list for proper housing to fit their needs?'

Daisy felt her face tingle hotly. He just didn't seem to understand. 'They would oppose any suggestion of moving,' she tried to explain. 'The house has been home to them for over forty years. Their only son grew up there. He was a soldier and he died in Belfast a few years ago. No matter how dilapidated the place is it's their roots with all their memories inside its walls.'

'Hmm,' was all she got by way of an answer and she gave up after that. If he couldn't see the situation for himself then it was useless banging her head against a brick wall trying to tell him.

The following call went without upset, the disabled woman 'over the moon' at being issued that day with a lifting hoist which would enable her family to help look after her more comprehensively.

But the next call was not so successful. Delia Ferguson had been diagnosed with cancer and today she looked terrible. Daisy knew the signs of a short-lived remission and her heart twisted for the woman she had come to admire so much over the past twelve months.

'I'm feeling sick with the chemotherapy,' Delia complained as Daisy sat with her on the sofa. 'I thought I might not take any more painkillers. See how I go.'

'Well, let me try an alternative first. I'll give you something to help with the nausea,' Josh offered gently. 'Do you have any family who can pop to the pharmacist for you.'

'I'll fetch it,' Daisy said quickly and reached out for the prescription.

'My son, Marcus, might be home,' Delia mumbled awkwardly, glancing at Daisy.

Daisy knew that Marcus was hardly likely to return. He'd reacted badly to his widowed mother's illness and had been consistently absent from home, which was why she had decided to call more frequently over the last few months.

Josh asked about the son as they sat in the car afterwards. Daisy explained yet again, but she was beginning to feel as though she was continually defending her patients against a barrage of criticism.

'Surely Marcus should be involved more?' Josh said incredulously. 'Has no one talked to him about the possible consequences of his mother's illness?'

'Delia has asked us not to,' Daisy said with a helpless shrug. 'And the district nursing team and your father have respected her wishes.'

'How old is the boy?'

'Seventeen. He's just left school.' Daisy wondered what was coming next.

'No job?'

'No, but he's a bright lad–'

'In which case he probably suspects something is going on that he doesn't know about.' An angry frown spread across Josh's forehead. 'Look, he's seen his mother develop her illness – and progressively become worse. He has no work, no father and without a doubt must be suffering from insecurity. Secretly he fears the loss of his mother – the possibility of which everyone refuses to talk about.'

Josh shook his head and gave an impatient sigh. 'This is ridiculous, Daisy; he should be counselled.'

This time Daisy's anger flared. 'But we can't go against Delia's wishes. Besides, you hardly know the family – it's a complicated situation, a very sensitive one.'

'True.' The passenger in the seat beside her shifted restlessly in the confined space and the car rocked with his weight. 'Marcus might very well be the kind of lad who can't cope with the truth but then again he just might. I know what I would want in his position. The truth.'

She hesitated, wondering at his certainty. It was almost as though he knew Marcus and that wasn't possible. She shrugged. 'Maybe. But even so … the decision doesn't lie with us. We can't interfere without Delia's permission.'

'Daisy...' He looked at her intently. 'You're seeing all this through Delia's eyes. You aren't giving validation to Marcus's feelings. I'm not criticising but I have to point it out. The root of the trouble is their relationship and everyone is ignoring it because of the cancer.'

Daisy was furious. How could he make such a judgement after just one visit? How could he take on the role of judge and jury? But, yet again, she hesitated, a deep-seated instinct within her telling her to remain silent for the moment.

The grey eyes were determined again. 'I would like to talk to Mrs Ferguson and then to Marcus at a later stage. I take it you aren't going to oppose me?'

Her loyalty to Delia made her want to object to any interference at this point in time. The poor woman had enough to contend with without family battles on top. But Josh was the doctor and whatever he said went.

'Of course not. I think you're wrong–' she pushed back the cold anger which threatened in her voice '–but it's not up to me. I'll provide you with the details of Delia's medical history in the form of the care plan.'

He nodded, pausing. 'I'm sorry you feel this way. But I will study all the information

44

before I talk to them.' He hesitated, his frown easing out. 'Let's take it one step at a time for now.'

The drive back to the surgery was, not surprisingly, a silent one. They said a polite goodbye and she watched him climb out of the car, just catching a muttered oath about cars being made like sardine cans these days.

His tall, rangy body was a head and shoulders above everyone else. His black hair and deep tan caused several women to look in his direction, as she was able to observe surreptitiously from the car.

Unexpectedly he turned to look back. Catching his gaze, she made a fumbled wave only because she'd been caught in the act. Hurriedly she jammed on the engine, glancing in her mirror to pull away with an embarrassing screech of tyres.

'Idiot,' she muttered to herself.

Her nerves were jangling as she approached the comfortable red brick house, with the two over-large chimney pots, which was home. She prayed that Uncle Toby wouldn't ask her too many questions about her day. He would wheedle out of her something about Josh – and she wasn't sure exactly what it might be.

The next morning Daisy fitted in an early call to her thyroid patient. Kathleen Ferry sat on

45

a piano stool beside her baby grand piano in the Edwardian drawing room, watching Daisy take her blood pressure. 'Poor Dr Cameron. Do you think he'll recover completely?' she asked.

Daisy hesitated as she inflated the rubbery cuff around her patient's plump arm. 'I hope so. We all hope so, naturally.'

'What a clever girl you were. Such presence of mind. Peter and I were so impressed.

'Peter?' Daisy was distracted as she read the gauge.

'Mmm. My nephew. The young man who was with me in the surgery the day Dr Theo collapsed, just after you said hello. Peter's a photographer and works in London and is taking some photos of Summerforde because we're so steeped in history.'

'How interesting.' Daisy was only half listening as she concentrated on the reading and the rather high figure.

'We both said if it hadn't been for you … well, I should hate to think what would have happened.'

Daisy frowned as she listened through the stethoscope to the blood forcing its way through the main artery. 'I wouldn't be much of a nurse if I dithered, would I?' She smiled. 'You say you've been feeling dizzy lately? How long is it since you've had a blood test?'

Kathleen Ferry frowned as Daisy helped

her up from her piano stool and into an easy chair. 'About eight months, I think. Yes, Christmas-ish time, I believe.'

'Then I suggest a test. I'll come in again and take one for you after I've checked with the doctor.'

Just as Kathleen was about to speak the door opened behind them and a man walked in. 'Which doctor?' Kathleen persisted, so worried that she forgot to make introductions.

'Oh, Dr Cameron's son. He's taken over for a while whilst his father is recovering. Dr Keen's out of action, I'm afraid, with a broken leg.' Daisy smiled at the young man.

Her patient frowned. 'Let me see ... he's the researcher, isn't he? Plays about with bugs and viruses and things. I hope we won't catch any of them!'

'Aunt Kathleen!' Peter Ferry arched thick blond eyebrows. 'You'll embarrass this young lady.'

'Your aunt's right,' Daisy laughed, aware of the handsome young man's embarrassment. 'He is a researcher. But I can assure you he's left all his bugs back in Florida – safely locked in freezers.'

Looking happier, Kathleen suddenly remembered to make formal introductions and Daisy and Peter shook hands. He was tall and very fair, she noticed, with roaming blue eyes, and he wore clothes which made him look very arty. She had visited Kathleen for a long time now but had never seen him before. It was good to know there was someone Kathleen could call on and Daisy made a mental note to write down his name in the care plan just in case they needed to contact a relative at any time.

'Well, I must be off,' Daisy sighed, packing her bag.

'I'll see you out.' Peter Ferry opened the door for her. 'Miss – er... Nurse ... what on earth do I call you? You don't look a bit like a nurse at all! Too young and too pretty!'

Daisy laughed, her green eyes sparkling at the teasing flattery. 'As it happens, just Daisy will do. Bye, Kathleen. See you soon.'

In her car, Daisy wound down the window and to her surprise Peter poked his head in, grinning. 'Daisy, will you be able to check my blood pressure too? I'm sure it's right up at the moment.'

She burst into laughter again, his teasing not deserving a sensible answer, and started the engine and waved. As she drove back through Summerforde to the surgery in the high street her mind easily dismissed the personable young man who had flirted with her. It flew instead to the deep grey eyes which seemed indelibly imprinted on her memory.

It was illogical to keep thinking about Josh Cameron, she told herself angrily. She hadn't forgotten that he had rudely warned her to keep out of family matters and was insensitively undermining her rapport with her patients by questioning her judgement.

But, nevertheless, she couldn't help recalling those wonderful grey eyes and the smile which made her feel as if sunlight had softly brushed her face.

Lunch having been taken swiftly, in the form of two fresh prawn sandwiches on the quay, Daisy headed back to the surgery and her meeting with Josh at one-thirty.

He was waiting for her as usual and, with no mention of the previous day, climbed in her car with a nod and a smile.

Daisy drove, rather quickly, to the block of flats on the east cliff. The English Channel lifted and heaved like an angry rollercoaster as they ducked their heads in the breeze, pausing to cast a windswept look over the beautiful view. The wind whipped white foam on waves which curled and dived in perpetual motion.

The lift took them to the eighth floor. Daisy led the way along the brightly lit corridor and rang the doorbell of Daniel Downey's apartment.

Josh had Daniel's care plan and his case in his hand as he stretched his long arm out immediately to the twenty-two-year-old. 'I hope you don't mind me calling with Daisy, Mr Downey. I'm Josh Cameron, standing in for my father who has been taken ill.'

Daniel Downey glanced at Daisy nervously. She gave him an encouraging smile. Her soft green eyes seemed to smooth the way for Daniel to open the door and allow them into the luxury flat. She had explained to Josh that the apartment had been left to Daniel by his widowed mother who had died a year ago. Daniel showed them to a room which overlooked the sea, but the blinds were drawn enough to obliterate the breathtaking view.

'I was wondering, while Daisy changes your dressing, if you would allow me to catch up on some info?' Josh asked in a deep, friendly voice.

Daisy carefully eased off the old dressing, then washed her hands and came back to slit open a saline pack. Theo Cameron had called in response to an SOS from the caretaker the week before his heart attack. Daniel had burnt his arm badly on the cooker but refused hospital treatment.

Josh glanced across and Daisy met his eyes. The wound was taking time to heal and Josh stood up to examine it, finally giving her a swift nod to clean and replace the stained dressing with a fresh one.

Daniel provided a few details willingly enough, but Daisy couldn't help noticing that his face was gaunt and his brown hair uncombed.

'This is a beautiful apartment,' Josh complimented, casting his eyes around the room. 'It reminds me of a place overlooking the ocean that I stayed in in Florida.'

'What were you doing in Florida?' Daniel asked, his eyes showing a faint spark of interest.

'I've been working in medical research. To be specific, on a new treatment for gastrointestinal disorders initially pioneered by a doctor in Australia.'

Daniel's face grew alert as Daisy finished his dressing, rolled down his shirtsleeve carefully and finally peeled off her disposable gloves. He said shyly, 'I'm hoping there might be some new research on my condition – if you know what I mean.'

Josh nodded slowly. 'Would you like to tell me something about yourself?'

To Daisy's surprise, the introverted young man began to explain his depression, which had led to psychotherapy treatment and antidepressants. She had tried everything she could to persuade him to communicate over the few months she had known him prior to the burn. But all endeavours had ended with a firm shut-down.

'You enjoy listening to cassette tapes, Daniel?' Josh asked gently. On a table beside the chair were a set of headphones and Daisy realized they had caught Josh's eye.

Daniel nodded and gestured to a library of

cassettes and CDs at the far side of the room.

'I've some tapes made by a doctor, a lady I first came across in Australia whilst I was working out there for a brief spell,' Josh said slowly. 'She has researched depression and understands that people who suffer from these illnesses cannot always travel to the doctor's for help. So she decided to make the journey into their homes herself by means of a cassette tape or CD. Perhaps you'd care to listen to one?'

The young man nodded, but shrugged with a lassitude that Daisy felt had deepened each time she saw him. She said as much to Josh when they left the apartment, explaining that the twin blow of family bereavement and his failed degree at university was, she suspected, the root of the trouble.

'Has he lost weight?' Josh asked as they climbed into the car.

'I think so. He refuses to be weighed.'

Josh nodded. 'I'd like to wean him off the antidepressants. They were only given as an initial month's supply, yet he's had four repeat prescriptions.'

Daisy sighed. 'Your father resisted giving them to him, but twice was called out when he suffered panic attacks and hyperventilated.'

Josh studied the notes. 'OK,' he murmured to himself, 'we'll see what we can do.'

He glanced up at Daisy. 'He likes you. He trusts you, doesn't he?'

She felt her cheeks redden. 'Actually, I've been finding it rather hard going,' she admitted reluctantly. 'I'm not sure whether he does trust me. And there's something else ... silly, I suppose...' Her colour deepened even more as she tried to explain.

'Not silly, go on.'

'Just this feeling, really. I'm worried about him, worried about his co-ordination, his thought processes, not particularly the burn itself. I just have serious doubts that he can cope on his own sometimes.'

Unexpectedly, he nodded. Brown fingers flicked through the care plan again. 'He was recently assessed by the outpatient psychiatrist at St Margaret's. To be reviewed in six months. Would you like me to get him in before that?'

Daisy hesitated. 'Yes, if possible. I'm probably making a mountain out of a molehill...'

He grinned. 'Not at all. A good nurse's intuition.'

She found herself unable to hide her deepening blush. He stared at her for a long while before he said softly, 'Would you like to come with me to see Theo this evening?'

Daisy started. 'With you?'

He nodded. 'United front and all that.'

'Oh, I see.'

'Theo would appreciate it. They moved

him today into a side ward which is far more private. I thought it would save you a journey if I picked you up.'

'Do you know where I live?' she asked hesitantly.

Josh nodded. 'I took the liberty of asking Helen. I'll have a quick shower and will be with you by seven-fifteen – I moved into the flat above the surgery last night so it will only take me five minutes to get to you.'

'You've left your mother on her own?' The question was out before she could stop herself.

'Helen has a house guest – a cousin who's come to stay for a few weeks while she's looking for a new job. They don't want me hanging around under their feet all the time.'

The thought forced its way across her mind like a slowly spreading stain of ink on blotting-paper – was he already avoiding the responsibility of his mother, palming the duty off on a relative?

Uncharitable, she knew, but all the same the doubts were there, mingled in confusion with the strange pleasure she had felt when he had asked her to go with him this evening – before he had explained that it was his father's wish to see her.

CHAPTER THREE

'Dressing up to the nines for a hospital visit, aren't you, my girl?' observed her uncle wryly.

Daisy tried to ignore the remark as she frowned into the mirror, attempting to coil her dark hair into a soft navy polka-dot scarf.

Her uncle wasn't looking at her but, dressed in his old dungarees and tilting his sea-cap, he ambled to the window, squinting out onto the road.

Daisy was wearing her new calf-length navy silk dress with its tiny white spots and her navy pumps to match. Why shouldn't she wear something attractive to brighten up Theo's day? Then, blushing guiltily, she admitted to herself that it wasn't for Theo's sake that she had taken so much trouble this evening, and the worst of it was that her uncle had guessed too.

'Here's your young man,' he announced, hurrying to the front door.

'Uncle Toby, he's not my–' Daisy stopped with a frustrated sigh because she realised she was addressing an empty room. Hurrying after him, she arrived in the hall in time to see Josh standing there, a wide grin on his face.

He was dressed in a short-sleeved pale blue shirt and dark trousers and looked completely relaxed as he strolled in, holding out his hand.

'You'll be Theo Cameron's boy, I suppose,' muttered her uncle, taking the hand and shaking it.

Inviting Josh in was just what she had hoped to avoid. An interrogation would follow and at best they would be delayed, at worst they would never leave the house at all!

'Like a beer before you go?' Uncle Toby asked, avoiding her eyes and she knew why – because murder was written in them.

'Sounds tempting,' Josh grinned. 'But I'm driving, thanks all the same.'

'We should go now,' Daisy protested, blushing under Josh's amused gaze.

'You fiddle with your hair first.' Her uncle pushed Josh into the front room. 'I'll entertain our guest.'

Daisy had no doubt that he would. The last thing she saw was a rueful gleam in Josh's grey eyes.

Sighing, she retreated and retrieved her lost scarf and tried to tie back her disorderly waves. No easy task when her fingers seemed to be going in all directions except the right one.

It was finally half an hour before she slipped into the Mercedes beside Josh. Most annoying was the smile on his face, unscathed as he seemed from his encounter with her uncle.

'Now I know where you derive your looks – dark hair, tawny skin, green cat's eyes – your mother was French, I hear?' He confirmed her suspicion that Uncle Toby had chronicled the family history in the space of thirty minutes.

'Don't look so disapproving; I was fasc- inated!' He started the car and gave her a rueful grin. 'Can you sing too?'

Daisy found herself laughing at his teasing. 'Only for my supper, or, at least, when I'm cooking it – or in the bathroom. Uncle Toby tells me I have the perfect bath-tub voice.' She looked across and met his eyes, which were twinkling with humour. 'And what other gory details did he manage to divulge?' She suddenly realised, with a small jolt of surprise, just how much she was already enjoying being alone in his company.

Josh chuckled. 'Don't worry, he didn't spill the beans. I was hoping he might let out some deep dark secret which I could hold over you.'

She smiled, a lazy, satisfied smile. 'That's a relief, then.'

'Have you any secrets in your life, Daisy?' he asked, suddenly serious, and she wished just for a moment that she had one.

'Not really … life's been pretty straightfor- ward on the whole. Uncle Toby's a darling.

He looked after me when my parents went on tour – they were completely wild in their early days, apparently, in Paris in the swinging sixties. Fell in love at first sight–'

'Ah, now there's a rarity,' he interrupted with an ironic arch of dark eyebrows. 'Personally I think people can make one hell of a mistake imagining something like that.'

Her mouth suddenly felt dry. She ran her tongue over her lips. 'Well, I believe in it,' she said quietly, fumbling for her safety belt as they drew up in the car park. 'Falling in love worked for my parents–'

'And you believe the same thing will happen to you?' His voice held a hint of mockery.

'Why not? What's wrong with falling in love?'

He shrugged, looking at her with a wry smile. 'It's not something, as a bachelor, I've spent a great deal of time thinking about.'

She felt a fool and blushed, groping around again for the release catch of the safety belt.

He leant across her. 'Here, like this…'

Somehow her fingers gripped his wrist unintentionally and she took in a breath as the strong tendons tightened beneath her touch.

He eased away her nervous fingers, twisting them slowly in his own as heat flooded her body. For a moment she was breathless, held in the spell, his fingertips tracing a path slowly along the soft curve of her bare arm,

58

somehow finding their way into her hair, undoing the silk scarf and letting the thick abundance slide slowly around her shoulders.

'You've wonderful hair, Daisy. Beautiful. Eyes a man could lose his soul for...'

Even before he finished speaking his mouth had closed down on hers. His kiss, soft and enquiring at first, deepened as the smell and taste and feel of him sent her senses into a whirl. She opened her eyes briefly. He tilted her head forward and kissed her again.

Suddenly the belt clicked open at her side and he pulled her roughly into his arms. Blood raced like a drug through her veins and his eyes locked with hers, darker than ever, inviting and intimate.

'God knows but I've wanted to do this since the first moment I saw you,' he whispered.

She made a soft, startled sound and swallowed. 'I didn't think... I mean, we just don't hit it off...'

Smiling, he shook his head and kissed each eyelid. 'Oh, Daisy, I'm afraid we do, in a very physical way.'

'But ... but I don't believe in just ... just–'

'Physical attraction? You think a man and a woman need to want each other's minds as well as their bodies to be attracted to one another?'

Nothing could have brought her back down to earth more swiftly. She tried to wriggle upright but he held her and she took in his glittering eyes, the desire that filled them, and the ragged groan that softly parted his lips.

'Daisy, you're a wonderful, warm, sexy woman. The way you responded meant one thing only – that you wanted me just as much as I wanted you.'

His thumbs moved across her cheeks, pulling the flesh back, as, before she could deny him and to prove his point, he bent to kiss her again, his mouth burning feverishly against her own.

She wriggled again, but he pulled her closer and this time she didn't want to resist. She felt that she was drowning, catching a last sight of the real world before she sank below the surface of physical need.

What he had said was perfectly true.

From the first moment he had knelt beside her she had known. Deep, deep down in her heart she had recognised him as a lover.

He buried his face in her hair. 'Let go, Daisy...'

She wanted to ... oh, yes, she wanted to.

'That's better.'

She shook her head. 'It isn't...'

'Put your arms around me.'

'No...'

He curled them up and she let them stay there.

'I want to kiss you and I know you want to kiss me. Look at me, Daisy.'

Aroused and confused, she looked at him.

She never knew quite how she replied or why she let her fingers stray so wantonly into his dark, thick hair. But suddenly they were there and he was kissing her and the kiss seemed to go on and on, until she felt she might burst with the pleasure of it.

But she did remember afterwards almost dying of fright as the knock came on the window like a bolt out of the blue.

She could barely focus on the face outside the car as Josh muttered gruffly, 'Who the hell is that?'

He let her go and swivelled around in his seat. A red-headed boy of about eleven or twelve, dressed in a vivid green 'Save The Whales' T-shirt, grinned in at them. Josh stabbed the button to propel the window down.

The boy handed him a white car-park ticket. 'Dad says you can have ours 'cos there's still a lot of time left on it.'

Josh grinned and took it. 'Thanks. Like the T-shirt, by the way.'

The cheeky face disappeared and Daisy swallowed hard as Josh turned back to face her; she wondered how on earth he'd manage to be so cool when faced with those enquiring young eyes.

'That's what you call being caught red-handed,' he chuckled, lifting his eyebrows, fiddling with the ticket between his fingers and finally snapping it on the windscreen. 'Now, where were we?'

She felt a flush of heat rush up from her toes. 'No...' she began, and swallowed again.

'No, what?'

'Josh, this is a mistake...'

'You mean because of the lad!' He frowned at her. 'He's probably seen a lot more than two people kissing in a car, even in his short lifetime.'

'No, not because of the boy, because of us ... because this isn't right.'

He was looking perplexed. 'It was right enough a moment or two ago.'

She quelled the urge to deny it flatly because she knew – absolutely knew – that whatever had happened between them had been a kind of freak reaction – she couldn't explain it and perhaps she didn't want to. She lifted her eyes. 'You and I are poles apart.'

He shrugged dismissively. 'Poles apart we might be, but it doesn't alter the fact that it still happened. Daisy, I–'

'You needn't apologise,' she broke in, intending not to duck the fact that she had fully participated in what had happened between them, but she caught the flicker of a smile on his mouth.

'I wasn't going to apologise. I was going to

suggest we should give ourselves a little time to find out just how far apart we really are.'

Her face crimsoned. Trying to salvage the last vestiges of her pride, she nodded towards the hospital and muttered lamely, 'We had better hurry; visiting time's almost over.'

'Don't be evasive.' He pulled her round to face him. 'There's someone else, isn't there?'

She stared at him in surprise. 'Do you think I would have let you kiss me like that if there was?'

He looked long and hard into her eyes before giving the faint wry frown which suggested half belief, half doubt. 'I honestly don't know.'

She took a breath and licked her dry lips. 'That's right. You don't know anything about me, Josh. If you did, you wouldn't have to ask such a question.'

'You're telling me you're just an old-fash-ioned kind of girl who believes she's going to fall in love – and stay in love – for the rest of her life?'

How could he make love sound cheap? But somehow he had. She felt the warm flush of anger on her face. 'Which just goes to show I was right. You and I have nothing in common–'

'Haven't we?' he asked hurtfully, lifting a cynical eyebrow. 'You might have your precious scruples about everlasting love, Daisy, but you've got a very convenient memory too.'

She dropped her eyes to mask the pain and the realisation that if she didn't get hold of herself soon she would be in tears.

'Oh, hell,' he growled, and she looked away from him through the window, biting back the tears.

'It's late,' she mumbled, then flung open the door and, whilst she had her back to him, covertly wiped her eyes with the trembling back of her hand.

Under the circumstances, the visit went better than she expected.

With Theo a willing recipient of their attention, they managed a reasonable three-way conversation and Josh touched lightly on the subject of the practice, Daisy's heart missing a beat as he glossed over the few questions his father put to him. Eventually Theo's attention began to drift and his eyelids grew heavy; she met Josh's glance with a furtive nod and they eased their way from the bed.

Outside in the corridor Josh heaved a sigh as he looked back through the partition. 'He seems very vague.'

'Early days yet,' she said with a small sigh.

He turned away heavily and began to walk down the corridor. 'It's just not good enough.

The surgery is floundering in the Dark Ages. The time for change has come. Now, while Theo is away from it all. We need computers, a photocopier, a fax–'

Daisy tried to keep up with his long strides. 'But not behind his back. Speak to him when he's home.'

'You know he wouldn't co-operate.'

'But even if you introduced all these things,' she gasped desperately, 'Emily has had no computer training. You can't expect her to cope with new technology and keep up with reception work. It just isn't fair.'

At the car, he turned to look at her and the grim determination in his eyes frightened her. 'With all the changes in the health service, Theo's working methods are impractical, uneconomical, archaic.' He brought his clenched hand down with a thump on the roof. 'Don't look at me like that, Daisy. Better that I change them now while he's away from it. He'll come around; so will Emily. In the end it will be better for everyone.'

'But wait,' she implored as he turned to face her. 'Wait until he's better.'

'Don't fight me,' he said slowly. 'I would rather do this with you than without you, Daisy, but one way or another I'm going to do it.'

She swallowed, knowing he would. 'All I'm trying to point out,' she murmured rea-

65

sonably, trying to keep her voice steady, 'is that there will be teething problems to contend with. Eventually it will be your father who'll have to face them – or Emily, and she's stressed enough.' She added carefully, 'You won't be here.'

To her bitter disappointment he didn't disagree but merely said, 'Then we shall have to find trained staff, people who can.'

'But that would mean–'

'Expansion. Theo must expand to survive. He can't continue as he is. The workload is just too great.'

Did he realise how much Theo had always resisted going into partnership? she wondered incredulously. He was the last of the old school. The family doctor who knew all his patients from birth to adulthood, their children and their children's children. He believed in the system and had maintained all his working years that he would never convert to the 'conveyor belt', as he called it.

'Anyway,' Josh added heavily, 'I'd appreciate it if you just kept all this under your hat for a while.'

She felt sick inside. What could she do? She was helpless to intervene. The trouble was that she was too close to the Camerons, had become a friend over the past two years – a big mistake.

In training she had been taught never to become too involved with a patient but to keep objective. No one had ever warned her of involvement with the GP. Except perhaps Uncle Toby! How right he had been to voice his concerns in the early days when she had helped the Camerons, Helen with her shopping and the new appliances which would eventually make her disabled life easier and Theo with the running of the surgery. Well, there had been no one else on hand, least of all the wandering hero now sitting beside her!

'Come on, I'd better get you back,' he murmured, and opened the car door. She slid in and watched him walk around to his own side. As the Mercedes slid off, she felt too confused to try to make conversation, and when the two chimneys of the house appeared on the darkening skyline she almost breathed a sigh of relief.

As she went to get out, he gripped her wrist. 'Tonight doesn't make us enemies, does it, Daisy?'

She understood what he meant. 'No, Josh. I just have to have time to think.'

He nodded and let her go. But as she went to close the door behind her he stopped her. 'Daisy, I would like to see Delia Ferguson. Can I leave you to arrange it for me?'

Suppressing her desire to ask him how he thought he would manage the installation of a computerised system if he couldn't pick up the phone and dial a local number, she shrugged. 'Is it urgent? I mean, what sort of time?'

'Preferably this week after evening surgery. Whenever is convenient.'

She took a step back, shivering a little in the cool air. 'Goodnight, Josh.'

He hesitated, and the sound of the engine running drummed in her ears. 'I meant what I said about talking, you and I.'

She nodded. But what good was talking? They were poles apart in just about everything except...

She heaved the door to and watched the car purr off until it disappeared from sight. She remembered clearly the way his skin and hair had felt beneath her fingers – rough and powerful and deliciously alive – and the way she had trembled in his arms when he had kissed her.

The following day Daisy met with Emily first thing, and, as Josh joined them, she managed, with superhuman effort, to keep her mind on the patients they were discussing.

Her morning rounds completed, she met him after morning surgery, keeping her conversation brief and to the point whilst driving them across Summerforde to the single call she had reserved for the afternoon.

He said nothing about yesterday and nor did she. How very civilised, she thought, wondering if she had dreamt it all. But a dream couldn't have left such an ache inside her and that was what she had – an indescribable ache. Unconsciously, after she'd stopped the car, she folded her arms around herself in a protective gesture.

She only realized what she was doing when he reached across and tugged out her hand and squeezed it. 'Friends?' he asked.

Did that mean he regretted what he had said yesterday? she wondered.

Her undoing, of course. She felt terrible. Worse. Yesterday flooded back ... everything flooded back as his touch tingled on her skin.

He let her hand go, smiling briefly at her. 'Come on; let's see our little spinster.'

Peter Ferry opened the door and gave her a wide smile, his blue eyes going to the tall, dark man accompanying her.

'Peter, this is Dr Josh Cameron.' She made the introduction carefully, keeping her tone light.

The two men shook hands and after a brief exchange of words they walked into Kathleen's drawing room to find her playing her baby grand piano. Daisy noticed with some alarm that she was bathed in perspiration and looking very waxy.

'Polonaise in C?' Daisy asked as Kathleen stopped playing and patted her forehead with a tissue.

Kathleen's tired eyes lit up. 'You recognised it! My playing can't be too bad, after all.'

'It's always a treat,' Daisy said gently. 'You play beautifully. I recognise every piece.'

'That's because you've a good ear for music, my dear.' Kathleen sat down in an easy chair, her eyes going up to Josh.

Daisy made the introductions and allowed herself a small smile as Josh complimented Kathleen on her playing, bringing a glow to the spinster's pale face.

'So, we'll begin by taking a little of your blood.' Josh smiled and Kathleen Ferry lifted up her arm without hesitation. Afterwards, Daisy stemmed the tiny red prick of blood with cotton wool.

'All done.' Josh removed the syringe and Daisy could see that their patient was captivated by his smile – not the first, she reflected, to be charmed by its brilliance.

Daisy entered up the care plan, mildly distracted as she listened to Josh's deep voice discussing the problems of Kathleen's thyroid condition.

Peter suddenly said in her ear, 'Have you a minute or two, Daisy, whilst Dr Cameron is checking my aunt?'

Thinking it was something he wished to discuss with her regarding Kathleen's condition, she allowed herself to be drawn to one side.

'It's simply that I'm taking some shots of Summerforde over the next few weeks and I wondered if you might like to step in as a model for me,' Peter Ferry said in a whisper.

Daisy laughed softly. 'I don't think I'd make a very good model, Peter. I wouldn't know the first thing about it.'

He grinned. 'That's just it. I don't want sophisticated poses. I want a real live Summerforde woman who expresses the character of the town.'

She shook her head, but before she could say anything he slipped an arm around her shoulders. 'I'm serious, Daisy. You're so right for what I want. Shots of the quay, for instance. Lobster pots and sunsets.'

Suddenly conscious of the silence in the room and the weight of his hand on her shoulder, she shrugged. 'I'll think about it.'

'How are you feeling, Kathleen?' Daisy asked, refusing to meet Josh's questioning eyes.

'Oh, better some days. But I'm so terribly tired. Sometimes it takes all my energy just to play the piano.'

'We'll soon get you right,' Josh said quietly, packing his case. 'I'll drop your blood sample off at Pathology today. Hopefully we should have the results through soon.'

'It's been delightful meeting you, Dr Cameron. I do hope you're going to stay for a while,' Kathleen murmured, glancing purposefully at Daisy.

Deeply embarrassed, Daisy looked away as Josh explained that he was only in England temporarily. Not for the first time Daisy wished that Kathleen were just a little less forthright, but finally they said their goodbyes and walked outside to the car.

Peter called from the doorstep, 'Don't forget to let me know, Daisy!'

She nodded, ridiculously aware that she was blushing.

In the car Josh's profile was set, his chin firmly out, his mouth drawn in a straight line.

'Is there something wrong?' she asked, sensitive to the strained atmosphere.

'I might well have asked you that.'

She felt the icy edge to his voice and glanced at him with a frown.

'I'm sorry, I don't understand.' Then enlightenment dawned as she realised what he meant. 'Oh, if you're referring to what Peter and I were discussing, it had nothing to do with Kathleen; just a personal matter.'

'Kathleen didn't seem to think so,' he muttered irritably. 'She kept peering back at you two over my shoulder.'

Daisy couldn't help but laugh. 'Oh, Kathleen's a wonderful lady, but too curious for her own good sometimes.'

'As is most of the female sex,' was the dry comment she received in return.

72

'Now who's thinking negatively?' she spluttered, and was relieved to find him smiling with her.

'Turn right for the path lab,' he said, pointing, and she realised that she had almost overshot the entrance to the hospital.

They managed to park right outside and Josh hurried in while she waited. When he returned he looked more cheerful. 'They're going to hurry it up for me. I think her myxoedema needs reassessment. Kathleen has all the external signs – cold, dry skin and hair which is extremely thin and brittle. I may have to increase her maintenance dose considerably.'

He paused as Daisy nosed the Escort into the flow of traffic. 'You obviously know them well?' he asked casually as he slipped a long arm around the back of her seat.

Daisy glanced at him with a frown. 'I've known Kathleen for the two years I've been with your father. You'll find all the details there in her care plan.'

'Hmm.'

She smiled. 'Peter I met only recently, if that's what you're wondering – which is, of course, not written up in the notes.'

He shrugged. 'Just curious. You two seemed pretty cosy.'

She laughed. 'I hardly know him. He's a photographer. Today he asked me if I'd pose for a few photos.' She giggled at his expression. 'Not what you're thinking, though!'

'Unusual chat-up line,' he muttered grimly.

'I think he's quite genuine. The trouble is I haven't time – and anyway, I'm not very photogenic.'

He pulled a face. 'And what makes you say that?'

'Oh, I've lived with me for quite a long while. Had a chance to study the mug shots.'

He laughed. Then his smile faded as she pulled on the brake outside the surgery. 'I'd say he knows exactly what he's talking about,' he murmured, lifting the ends of her hair from her shoulder.

She trembled. 'Josh–'

'It's all right,' he growled, dragging away his hand. 'I must get in for evening surgery.' He got out of the car and walked around to her window, bending low as she wound it down. 'Daisy ... when are we going to get together?'

She shook her head, her heart thumping. 'I don't think that's a very good idea, Josh – in the circumstances.'

He grinned, eyeing her with amusement. 'Personally I think the circumstances are very conducive. Think on it, Daisy. I never take no for answer.'

CHAPTER FOUR

The Summerforde health centre was a stark and disturbing contrast to the antiquated Cameron practice. A maze of white walls and smoky windows, it reflected a character-less sky and even less inviting interior when Daisy arrived there on Thursday morning, hurrying along the streamlined, colour-coded corridors, thankful not to have to make too many frequent visits on behalf of her two diabetic patients.

Wondering, after checking their records, whether or not she should stop to pick up a special mattress she had ordered for one of them, she decided she might as well. Leaving the office, she headed along a corridor to the storeroom. A fair-haired girl bumped into her as they both reached the required room at the same time.

'Oops ... Daisy! How are you?'

'Karen! Fine, thanks.'

The two district nurses giggled, realising they were both intent on making a swift visit. Pushing her tousled fair hair back from her eyes, Karen Beech tugged Daisy into the storeroom and closed the door with a sigh. 'Ah, that's better. Nice and quiet in here.

Now, how's life with you? Pretty good, I hear.'

Daisy smiled ruefully. 'And what have you heard?'

'Oh, a bit of this and a bit of that.' Karen smiled tantalisingly. 'But mostly that Theo Cameron's long-lost son has turned up and he's tall, dark and handsome – and single!'

Daisy felt herself beginning to blush and quickly gathered her scattered train of thought. 'As a matter of fact the grapevine has it all wrong this time. He's short, wears specs ... and has a wife and at least three kids at home.'

The other nurse groaned. 'Daisy, don't tease. Come on, what's he really like?'

Daisy shrugged. 'Oh, I'm not sure yet. Full of new ideas ... he wants to model the surgery on something like this, heaven help us.'

Her friend scowled. 'Tell him from me there are serious disadvantages, especially when the computer breaks down and we have to sort out the muddles or a receptionist hasn't a clue what we're talking about because she doesn't know the patient personally.' She waggled an empty envelope in front of her. 'Like this. There's a repeat prescription missing from old Mr Drury's care plan and no one seems to know anything about it.'

Daisy nodded in sympathy. 'At least Theo and Emily know all the patients. Josh is finding our personal filing system a little hard to decipher, though.'

'Ooh ... first names already, is it?' Karen grinned teasingly.

Daisy couldn't hide her blush this time. 'Well, he's not entirely unapproachable,' she retorted defensively and, to cover her embarrassment, glanced at her watch. 'Better go. I'm late already.' Then, seeing the mattress she had come for stuffed under a shelf, she moved quickly across the room and tugged it out.

Too close for comfort, she decided as she bundled her armful into the car. Karen, who'd missed her vocation as a gossip columnist, was bound to assume the worst.

She made several more visits before lunchtime, trying to erase the idiotic notion of an affair with Josh from her head. But she thought about it for a moment, half-seriously. He'd made it patently clear that he wanted an affair and just as clearly he had no intention of settling down. What was it he'd called her? An old-fashioned girl with scruples? Well, what was so wrong in believing in love and marriage?

She had realised with Ned Asher that sex and a fling was all he really wanted and she didn't blame him now when she looked back. But how empty their relationship would have been without love.

She'd seen it with her parents. Love had

held them together in the good times and throughout her mother's long illness. That kind of love was what she wanted and what she had been waiting for – perhaps it was an old-fashioned notion. But it had worked for thousands of years before Josh Cameron set foot on this planet! And no doubt it would go on working for thousands of years more.

No, she didn't want an affair, but she was tempted ... oh, God, yes, she was. And who was to say she couldn't change his mind...?

Ridiculous even to think of it. But she was, wasn't she? Thinking of it?

Back at the surgery, Emily passed Daisy the phone and she called Delia. To her surprise, Delia agreed to the meeting with Josh without hesitation.

'Problems?' asked a deep voice from behind her, and she jumped.

Emily laughed as she looked up from the desk. 'Guilty conscience, Daisy?'

He smiled in wry amusement and she swallowed purposefully, absolutely sure that her face recorded every syllable of her thoughts. She thrust the note she had made into his hand. 'Delia, tomorrow, seven-thirty,' she mumbled, and licked her dry lips.

Long, dark lashes fanned his cheeks as he studied her scrawled details, then the grey eyes came up warmly to catch her stare. 'No problems?'

'No. None. She seemed happy enough to agree.'

He nodded slowly. 'I thought the suggestion might come better from you. Are you OK? You look a bit pale.'

She managed an over-bright smile. 'Just a bit of a rush this morning, that's all. Er ... if you don't need me...?'

'I wouldn't say that.' He looked at her hungrily. A suggestive light flickered in the depths of his eyes as he stared at her, one eyebrow lifted fractionally above the other.

'After lunch, then,' she muttered, completely fazed, hurrying out before her face lit up like a beacon, wondering if she had imagined the question written in his expression or if it had been the reflection of her own decidedly wanton thoughts this morning.

After a hurriedly eaten sandwich at home with her uncle she returned to collect Josh and begin their calls, but not before she had applied a soft pink to her lips and a shadow of mascara to her long black lashes for good measure. Her hair, of course, made its own arrangements, for the black waves, once brushed down, only re-formed into their thick halo however she styled it.

Glancing in her driving mirror, she was relieved to discover that she appeared reasonably human. Her eyes, though – did they give her away? Sea-green, more luminous than usual, more sparkling, reminding her of the seeking pressure of firm lips, the tough, hard body against her breasts and the feel of the muscular shoulders and rich, dark hair through which she had run her fingers.

'Locked!' someone was shouting. To her surprise, she saw Josh standing on the pavement, stabbing a finger at the door. Five minutes of her life had just elapsed without her knowing it! The car was parked and she was sitting in it like a lemon.

'Oh … sorry!'

She flicked the catch and he slid in beside her, folding up his long legs, crunching his knees on the dashboard. She watched him lever himself into the seat, all arms and legs, lifting his case into the back, but not without first colliding with the headrests.

He grinned at her. 'Sorry, not used to sardine cans.'

She looked indignant. 'People's knees don't usually reach that far.'

'Which is a reasonable argument for taking the Mercedes next time,' he chuckled, in a final effort to get himself settled.

She had to admit that he looked uncomfortable. It wasn't her fault, though – it was, after all, a practical little car for her purposes.

'Rita Farley's nine-month-old delivered its breakfast onto my jacket and managed to christen my trousers all in one ear-splitting yell,' he told her as they started off. 'Big mistake wearing this sort of gear.'

She glanced at the immaculate grey suit with the tiny white stain on the shoulder. 'It is a bit over the top for general practice.'

'I failed to foresee I'd need a pinny when I packed.' With a struggle he slid an arm along the back of her seat. 'I was supposed to be at a conference somewhere on the other side of the world, remember?'

'Just one of life's little surprises,' she croaked as she felt his fingers wiggle in her hair and, with a clumsy clunk, jerked the car into third.

'Oops, you can throw that one away,' he grinned, and tugged back his hand. 'Better behave myself while you're driving.'

Blushing, she avoided clashing any more gears, though she had difficulty in concentrating as she felt his gaze.

'Mind that car!' he yelled suddenly as, just for a moment, she tried hitching down her skirt, which was riding way above her knee and on which his eyes had been fixed for the last five minutes.

She swerved. 'I saw it, thank you.'

He shifted uneasily. 'Could have fooled me.'

'I'd no idea you were such a nervous passenger.'

He stared at her with a wry smile. 'I was distracted. You shouldn't have such lovely legs. Do you know when you change gear they seem longer than ever?'

She stalled the car. 'Thank you very much,' she said, glowering, and waved in apology to the driver behind.

'Not at all.' He watched the car swerve around them and then leaned closer. 'This is cosy, isn't it?' And when someone blared his horn he added with decided calm, 'I could get quite addicted to living dangerously.'

Through each of the visits Theo's son sat and talked with the patients, his deep voice calm and resonant, his concerned interest in each of the different cases causing Daisy some surprise as she listened whilst her fingers worked automatically changing dressings and cleaning wounds. He was good. Very good. He didn't patronise and he wasn't smug.

She was impressed.

As they left the last patient she had to admit to herself that she'd initially formed a mental picture of a self-absorbed, career-addicted male who allowed nothing to get in the way of personal aims. Yet she hadn't witnessed anything but a kindness and compassion that came genuinely from the heart – unless – perish the thought – he was a brilliant actor and she a very poor judge of character.

As she was trying to reconcile her mental

differences, he glanced at his wristwatch and said, surprising her, 'How about calling in on the Adamses? We've time before you drop me back at the surgery, haven't we?'

Daisy lifted her foot from the accelerator, a reflex action to a trick question. 'Did you want to see them for a specific reason?'

'Forget it if you're too busy.' He folded his arms and considered the congested street ahead.

The red flag having been metaphorically waved, Daisy yanked down her indicator and turned right and right again in the direction of the Adamses'.

'Daisy, dear – and Dr Cameron!' Mrs Adams struggled to the door with her walking frame, welcoming them with one of her brightest smiles the moment she saw who was with Daisy.

Josh smiled back. She could almost feel its warmth reflected on Mrs Adams's face. 'Mrs Adams, I wonder if it's convenient to have a quick word?' He spoke smoothly, in a tone that would have gained him immediate entry to Fort Knox, Daisy reflected suspiciously.

A pot of tea and a plate of cookies materialised as they made space to sit on chairs that were cluttered with knitting and newspapers.

Josh devoured two of the cookies, gulped

back his tea, then produced a thick manila envelope from his case. 'Just take a quick look at this, will you?'

Mr Adams dutifully took it, opened it and read. His face was a blank as he passed it, eventually, to his wife, who said after a few moments, 'Very nice, Dr Cameron, but what's it all to do with us?'

'How would you like to have one just like it?' Josh asked intriguingly.

Daisy could restrain her curiosity no longer and inched forward in her chair to peep over Mrs Adams's shoulder. Mrs Adams held up the illustration for her to see.

'A bathroom suite just like I've always wanted,' she remarked, as though she had just won the football pools.

Josh grinned. 'I've made enquiries with the local borough council. I had a hunch you were entitled to a grant which is awarded to home owners who qualify under certain circumstances. If we can persuade the authorities of the need for a ground-floor bathroom all we need is planning permission.'

The room was silent. Finally Mr Adams, after digesting the shock news, shook his head. 'I couldn't be bothered with all that red tape, Doctor. Why, it takes me all my time to puzzle out our electricity bills. Planning permission and grants – you might as well be speaking a foreign language!'

Josh shrugged. 'I'll attend to all that for you. The most you'll have to do is provide the builders with a cup of tea now and then and put up with a bit of noise.'

Mrs Adams stared at the brochure. 'Dr Cameron, we've never asked for charity in all our lives. As much as I'd love a bathroom like this, I don't want charity.'

'A grant for improvement isn't charity,' Josh told her firmly. 'This is an entitlement only for those who qualify. Think it over. With luck you would have a new bathroom for the winter.'

'No one has ever offered help like this before,' the old man sighed.

Daisy realised that that was true. No one, except Josh, had ever considered it feasible that the Adamses would consider help, let alone accept it.

'Beginner's luck,' Josh shrugged as they left and climbed back into the car and Daisy stared at him accusingly. 'And anyway, I'm not sure if they'll go for it.'

'Oh, they'll go for it,' she assured him. 'You sold Mrs Adams the bathroom the minute you showed her the brochure.'

He grinned. 'I cheated a bit, but wasn't it worth it?'

Undecidedly, she started the car. 'Couldn't you have let me in on the secret beforehand?'

He eyed her curiously. 'You would have fought me.'

Her jaw fell. 'Of all the–'

'Think of the upset, you would have said. A lot of fuss and bother to two old people caught up in a lot of hoo-ha when they were perfectly happy the way they were. Er … just watch out for the crossing…'

She bit down on her lip and braked. Mothers and prams ambled across the road. 'You still should have told me. I felt an idiot just sitting there with my mouth open. They are my patients too.'

He nodded and looked suitably penitent. 'I apologise. It was a bit sneaky.'

'Sneaky and…' she sighed, grinding the gear-lever as she thrust it forward and glancing at him with resigned, silent admiration '…successful.'

He grinned his appreciation. 'In which case, what do you say to a little celebration?'

'Celebration?' She glanced at him suspiciously. 'Can you be more specific?'

A suitable time passed as he frowned thoughtfully, though she would have bet a week's wages that the apparent inspiration had long been planned. 'How about a drink? A nice quiet English country pub or a meal in town… Or, if you're feeling adventurous, a show?'

She eyed him with rueful amusement. 'All because of the Adamses?'

'Not entirely.'

'Well...'

'Er ... suppose we continue this discussion,' he muttered, gripping the seat as she took, rather inadvisedly, a corner too fast, 'when we aren't looping the loop.'

She straightened up the car calmly and smiled. 'You haven't seen anything yet.'

'Women drivers,' she heard him mutter.

It was only when she returned home and found Peter Ferry talking to her uncle that she woke up from the spell. Uncle Toby relinquished his guard of the front door with a grunt, and that, she decided, was enough to waken even Sleeping Beauty.

'Sorry,' Daisy apologised on behalf of her uncle. 'Do you want to come in, Peter?'

Peter Ferry ginned and shook his head. 'No ... I can see I've caught the household at the wrong time. I was just wondering about some shots of the quay. I'm down again soon. Can I ring you and make a date?'

Half-heartedly agreeing, more from a desire to go in and stand under the shower and dream about the other invitation she had had than from any desire to be a model, she watched the departure of the white Porsche from the gate with relief then fled upstairs to the bathroom.

Her mind was full of Josh as she stripped

and stepped under the cool water. He had asked her out – and she had not said yes. At least with her lips. With her heart, she had greedily accepted.

Closing her eyes, she let the water run over her, but it wouldn't wash away his image, or his scent, or his seductiveness. Would he ever get around to asking her again, she wondered, and made a secret resolve to drive more carefully next time he was a passenger.

Friday morning brought soft, summer rain.

Daisy hurtled into the surgery, brushing the moisture from her cheeks, to find Emily surround by cardboard boxes and a stranger on his knees by the electrical socket. 'All systems go,' the man yelled.

The object of everyone's attention, she saw, was a brand-new computer.

'Don't look so worried,' he joked, and sat down on Emily's chair with a satisfied sigh. 'I'll give you a few straightforward lessons,' he offered magnanimously, 'and leave you with the manual.'

Emily sank down on a stool, her face white. 'You'll have to go very slowly. I'm useless at machinery.'

Daisy could hardly believe her eyes. Josh had really been serious about the computers. But now? Today? Five minutes from opening the door?

The voice of Computer Man droned on,

spouting unidentifiable terms.

'You try to concentrate,' Daisy whispered as she bent down and squeezed Emily's tensed shoulder. 'I'll take the phone calls while you listen. Is Josh in yet?'

Emily gave a helpless shrug. 'I've tried the flat but he's not up there.'

'Maybe he's on a call,' Daisy muttered doubtfully, signing in the first two patients of the day. She answered the phone and, checking her watch, took a stream of messages. Then, just as she began to despair, Josh ambled in through the front door, holding it open for an attractive young blonde to follow in after him.

'Ah...!' Black eyebrows rose approvingly in the direction of Computer Man. 'Morning, Frank. Great. Any problems with the installation?'

Frank shook his head. Emily looked stunned as the phone began to ring again and Daisy shook herself into action once more and hurried over to answer it.

'Thanks!' Emily called, but Daisy barely heard as she made the appointment, warded off a late delivery of post and settled in the first patients.

When at last she took a breath and turned back to the little group huddled around the computer Josh extracted himself from the conversation and gave her the same brand of smile that had reduced Mrs Adams to marshmallow yesterday.

'I have to go, Josh.' She waved a hand in the general direction of the early-morning chaos. 'I'm late al–'

'Of course.' He looked abstractedly at his clamouring waiting room, at a woman and her three small children, the youngest of whom was waving a dripping lollipop over the neatly covered knees of the pensioner in the next seat.

'But what about Emily? She can't possibly cope. You've all these patients waiting and–'

'No problem.' He took her elbow and steered her out from behind the desk. 'Corinne,' he said, nodding towards the blonde who had arrived with him, 'is going to be with us until the change-over is complete. She's an experienced computer operator, so Emily can take her time and get used to the machine whenever she isn't busy. Don't worry, everything's in hand. Mrs James, would you like to pop along to my room?'

The woman grabbed her children and bundled them along the corridor. Josh smiled pleasantly at the remaining patients and said, 'Hi.'

The crisis unexpectedly over, Daisy fell silent. A new computer and a new computer operator all in one day – it was good going, even for Theo's son.

'I'll be off,' called Computer Man and Josh raised a hand.

'Thanks, Frank. You'll let me know when you're installing the others?'

'Sure will. Toodle-oo, all.'

In the silence that followed Corinne slipped demurely behind Emily's desk and began to tap away at the keyboard, eliciting an instant response from the hitherto inactive machine.

'Good, isn't she?' Josh murmured before glancing at his watch. 'Well, better let you go.'

Daisy gathered her case and, to the vague sound of the computer humming, made her way out of the surgery and into the morning air.

Idiot, she remonstrated with herself, unlocking her car and dropping with a sigh onto the seat. That was what came of underestimating someone like Josh. Grass never grew under his feet. She should have learned that by now!

It wasn't an easy morning.

Her disabled patient's lifting hoist jammed and she had to call out the engineers. Daniel Downey refused to allow her to change his dressing, languishing in the depths of a profound depression. She only remembered at the last minute to give him the cassette Josh had promised him, and even this gesture seemed inadequate when he seemed so poorly.

Much later and very reluctantly she returned to the surgery. Corinne was feeding the new machine, as dauntingly poised and beautiful as she had been hours ago, and Emily was by the old switchboard, her brow pleated in a frown as she covered the mouthpiece of the phone with her hand. 'It's Delia Ferguson,' she called over Corinne's blonde head. 'She was admitted half an hour ago. Suspected overdose.'

'Overdose?' Daisy stared, unable to take it in. 'But surely not Delia? She's the last person–'

At that moment Josh appeared. 'Delia?' he frowned and Emily repeated the message.

'Tell them I'm on my way,' he grunted, flying back into his room without a glance at Daisy, and she hesitated for a moment.

'Surgery's finished; there's no one left,' Emily said, reading her thoughts. 'Why don't you go with Josh? I'll cope here. I can always ring you at the hospital if something crops up.'

Josh appeared, throwing on a dark blue jacket. 'Sorry about lunch, Corinne. Can you rustle up a sandwich with Emily?'

The girl dredged up a smile. 'Oh, I suppose so.'

Daisy watched as a smile passed between them. Surprised that she could feel so excluded, she tried to ignore the stab of pain at her ribs. After all, she told herself reasonably as she followed Josh out, he was a striking man. A very striking man. Most women seemed visibly stunned when he smiled at them. What was one more on the list?

'I'll come with you, if you don't mind,' she said, and passed Emily her case to tuck away in safety.

Josh shrugged but he didn't object and Daisy found herself walking with him to the Mercedes, in unspoken acquiescence that they should take his car.

'I just can't understand why Delia would do something like this,' Daisy sighed as he unlocked the car and she slid in beside him on the cool leather seat. 'It's so out of character. How was she last night?'

'Meaning what? That I left her in such a distressed state that she would deliberately take an overdose?'

'Of course not. I wasn't implying that it was anything you said – or did.'

'It sounded like it.' He drove into the lane from the parking space behind the practice and nudged the nose of the car into the mainstream traffic. 'Because if you think I had anything to do with the overdose it doesn't say a lot for our working relationship – or your trust in me, come to that.'

He was angry – and she didn't blame him. If Delia's problem had been entirely distanced from his visit then he had a right to be annoyed, but she couldn't help thinking how odd it was that the overdose happened after he had seen her.

What if it had been unintentional, for example? What if Delia had been worried about something he'd said about Marcus? For, as much as Delia's illness had weakened her physically, she was still emotionally strong, just as long as she could put on a façade of normality for her son. And if Josh had threatened this in any way, who was to say what might have happened?

Delia, they were informed, was in a side ward. Josh found the sister in charge and disappeared with her, leaving Daisy to sit it out in the waiting room.

She was surprised to find, however, when she next glanced at her watch, that almost an hour had passed. Deep in thought, she'd been oblivious of time, and as she stretched her legs suddenly Josh's tall form emerged through the swing doors.

He looked tired and preoccupied and for a moment her stomach tightened.

'"She's as comfortable as can be expected" – to quote,' he sighed, leaning against the wall. 'At the moment she's too confused to tell us what happened, so the best thing is to let her settle.'

Daisy leant back in the chair and expelled a long breath. 'Thank God she's all right.' She looked up at him with a frown. 'What do you think happened?'

'I wish I knew.' He thrust a hand wearily through his hair. 'I keep going over all we said, trying to work it out. Still, I can't do anything more until tomorrow... Feel like coming in to see Theo?'

She sighed, got up and tugged her navy cardigan around her shoulders. 'Sure you want me with you?'

A flicker of recognition crossed his face. 'I'd appreciate it if we ... were discreet.'

Her mouth dropped open as she stared at him, but after a fairly indecisive wrestling match with her conscience and the vivid mental picture of Corinne at the computer and Emily's poor face this morning she shrugged. 'Have I any choice?'

'Not if you don't want to upset him.'

'You know I don't.'

'Well, then?'

'That's blackmail.'

He took her arm. 'No, it's not. It's common sense.'

Neither of them spoke again as they made their way to the ward and finally discovered Theo asleep in his chair in his blue and red striped dressing gown, a pillow stuck behind his head. His eyes slowly opened as they neared and he managed a grin. 'Well, bless my soul–' He tried to stand up but Josh saw how weak he was and laid a hand on his shoulder. Daisy bent forward to brush her lips against his cheek as he sank back into

95

the seat without putting up too much of a fight.

'Came to see what you're up to,' Josh joked, and pulled up a couple of grey plastic seats for them to sit on.

'Chance would be a fine thing,' Theo complained, and jabbed a finger at a limp leg. That, he said, was the worst offender, but the feeling had come back into his arm after physio.

The moment came, as Daisy had dreaded, when he enquired about the practice, and Josh gave an edited version, saying in answer to Theo's enquiry about Emily, 'Oh, we're rubbing along pretty well on the whole. No problems so far.'

'Secretaries like Emily are one in a million,' his father muttered, and Daisy felt her eyes drop. When she lifted them again she saw the strain on Josh's face and wondered how long it would be before Theo realised he was the subject of one impossible deception.

'Well, go on, say it!' Josh shouldered open the door as they left the ward.

'Say what?'

'That you think I've no right to do what I'm doing – keeping Theo in the dark.'

'It's not important what I think.'

'Don't be ridiculous.'

She stopped in her tracks. 'I'm not. You

want my silence in front of Theo but you grant me permission to voice my opinion privately?' She shook her head firmly. 'Thank you, but you've already made it quite clear what you think about my involvement in your parents' lives.'

'Oh, for heaven's sake, Daisy, that was before... I mean, we know each other better now. All I'm asking is that you bear with me. Trust me.'

In the silent corridor, Daisy thought she could hear her heart pounding out of her chest with anger. Trust him? After what had just happened? All she knew was that she had entered the deception too, albeit reluctantly. She'd deceived Theo by omission and that was just as bad, in her book, as outright lying.

CHAPTER FIVE

Of course Daisy regretted losing her temper afterwards, as she'd known she would, and so, predictably, she didn't enjoy her week-end.

Saturday morning she was on duty and, passing by the practice when she had finished, she was not surprised to see the front door firmly shut and no movement above from Josh's flat.

There was no formal surgery on Saturdays, just emergencies, and as she drove home she resisted the urge to go out of her way past the Cameron house just to see if the Mercedes was parked in the front drive. Why? Daisy asked herself. Why should she want to know where Josh was ... or, more honestly, who with?

Angry with herself for her foolish curiosity, she spent the rest of the day in the garden with her uncle at her heels and passed an uneventful Sunday, barely tasting the roast lamb she cooked for them both.

Monday came with cloudy skies – a fitting beginning to her morning, she decided as she ran over again the list of queries she had mentally listed for Josh.

'No Corinne?' she asked as she walked into the surgery, discovering Emily making coffee in the kitchen.

'Coming in late this morning. Hair-do, I think.' Emily sipped her percolated coffee and sighed. 'Lovely. Sit yourself down and have a cup.'

Daisy had arrived early, so she was grateful for the offer. She saw the computer manual lying open on the worktop and grimaced. 'How are the lessons going?'

Emily shrugged. 'Ghastly.' She flicked through the pages and closed the book with a sigh. 'I'm better on my own with the book, I think.'

'You can actually make sense of it?'

'More sense than I can of Corinne.' Her lips formed a wry smile as she asked curiously, 'Did you know she's a distant relative of the Camerons, second cousin removed or something? She's staying with Helen at the moment.'

Daisy shook her head slowly. 'No ... I'd no idea.' She caught Emily's inquisitive stare. 'I was wondering...'

'If she was his girlfriend?' Emily laughed. 'I'd be very surprised if she was Josh's type. Still, you never know these days.'

'No, that's true.' Daisy shrugged and lowered her empty mug thoughtfully. 'Well, this won't do. Lovely coffee. Thanks, Emily.' Standing up, she turned and walked straight into Josh.

'Good morning,' he said quietly.

Daisy knew she was scarlet. How long had he been standing there? Emily shoved a cup of coffee straight into his hands, meeting Daisy's embarrassed stare with a look that said he just might have overheard most of their conversation.

'No one arrived yet?' he asked, one dark eyebrow raised enquiringly.

'Weather's too good for visits to the doctor,' Emily murmured philosophically. 'Even the temporary residents pack away their holiday blues and save them until the rain literally drives them from the beach.'

Josh made a wry comment as Emily rinsed their mugs and Daisy dried them, neatly stowing away the paraphernalia of the coffee-break.

When Emily left them, Daisy looked up at him with a small, hesitant smile.

'Hello,' he said huskily, and hesitated for a moment before he stepped towards her and drew her into his arms. She didn't resist, melting into them eagerly, the incurable ache she had had under her ribs all weekend finally dissolving.

'Oh, Daisy, I've missed you,' he sighed and squeezed her to him.

Not half as much, she thought silently, as I missed you.

'I'm sorry. I'm sorry for dragging you into

this whole mess.' He cupped her face in his hands.

'I just feel so … so disloyal to Theo.'

'I know.'

Her hands rested on his shoulders. She wanted to push her fingers into his hair, feel its soft thickness. 'Oh, Josh, isn't there another way?'

He drew his hands down over her arms. 'I wish there was.'

She had finally accepted that, she supposed, but it still hurt. 'Josh, don't let's quarrel today – if we start talking about Theo and the practice it's bound to happen.'

He lifted her chin and pressed his mouth warmly against hers. Oh, God, she thought, I'm falling, despite everything; I've no control any more.

'I want to see you, Daisy. We need to talk.' He went to kiss her again as suddenly, from somewhere in the waiting room, came the first demanding shriek of a child.

He released her with a deep sigh and they stared at one another until, lifting his shoulders in defeat, he laughed. 'What was it I said about living dangerously?'

Laughing too, she foraged self-consciously in her pocket for a list she'd made last night. 'Before you disappear, I was going to ask you–'

'The answer's yes,' he interrupted teasingly and ducked as she lunged out at him.

'I'm serious, Josh.'

'And so am I.'

'Don't you ever give up?'

He shook his head. 'I've only just started.'

Saved by the same screaming child running down the hall as Emily called her back to her mother, Daisy had one more try.

'Josh, I'm worried about Daniel.'

He gave a rueful smile and grabbed her arm. 'Come on, then; talk to me as we go. Daniel Downey, you mean?'

'He won't let me in for more than a few minutes. Then there's the diazepam; he always wants more before his prescription is up. His movement and his speech aren't co-ordinated... Oh, I suppose I'm worrying for nothing.'

'Did you by any chance give him that cassette tape?'

She nodded, wondering how a cassette tape was going to change the course of Daniel's depression.

'You'd like me to call, I take it?'

'Please.'

'OK. I'll go as soon as I can.'

He dropped her arm before they reached Reception and when they arrived there the room was overflowing. He bent to haul up a crashing toddler and she found herself watching the dark, well-shaped head, the graceful movements of his large hands and supple brown fingers and the ripple of his shoulder muscles underneath the grey jacket.

Oh, she wanted him. And it was possible, all too easy, to fall into those arms, to be kissed and kiss back. But what then? How would her precious scruples help her when she was saying good-bye to him in a few months' time?

'Emily's wrong about those holiday blues,' he frowned. 'I think I'm going to have to postpone our afternoons for a bit. When I've finished this lot I'll have calls. Do you mind very much?'

'Of course not.' She listened to the general din and Emily's faint voice slowly subsiding under the rising volume. 'I'd better let you go.'

He grinned at her and whispered softly, 'I wish you wouldn't.'

She felt herself flush. 'Oh... What about Delia?'

'I'm collecting her at lunchtime, rather than waiting around for hospital transport.'

She nodded. 'That's thoughtful of you.'

He called the first patient into his room and was soon lost to sight as three people charged up at once.

She came to a decision as she left. Apart from the necessary weekly call on Delia, she'd leave him to work the case out for himself. After all, distancing herself was probably what she should have done in the beginning but, because she was losing objectivity, her judgement was impaired. And this, she knew, could have repercussions for everyone. Especially Delia.

Corinne Franks seemed a permanent fixture at the surgery.

It was as Daisy hurried in to call for her messages on Thursday that she found her with a subdued Emily at the desk, the air thick with tension.

'Hi!' she called breezily to break the silence as Emily sat grimly at the computer with a glazed expression.

Dressed in a short white summer dress, looking stunning but bored, Corinne lifted her eyes but barely made an acknowledgement. It wasn't so much the icy expression that was irksome, Daisy thought, smiling instead at Emily, but the indifference of the girl, as if she barely knew that anyone else existed on the planet.

'Daisy?' Josh's voice echoed from the hall and he hurried towards her. 'I've a Mr Stokes in my room, new patient, in a good deal of distress. He wears a drainage bag and he's due to go in for a prostate gland op shortly. I was just about to tackle a bladder irrigation when the police rang through and asked for a visit.'

Daisy knew Theo was on a registered list for emergency calls to the station, though it wasn't often that they called him. 'Do you want me to do the irrigation for you?' she offered, as clearly he had to choose between patient and call.

'It's your lunch-hour, isn't it?'

'Which reminds me, it's mine,' Corinne called, overhearing a snatch of the conversation, 'and we promised to go back and have a snack with your mother. You're coming with me, aren't you, Josh?'

He grimaced and thrust a fist at his forehead. 'Snakes alive, I'd forgotten Helen.' He shook his head in self-reproach, tight-lipped and obviously annoyed with himself. 'You'll have to make my apologies, Corinne. Tell Helen some other time, hopefully, when we aren't too pushed.' He glanced back at Daisy, apparently oblivious to the disappointment in his receptionist's eyes. 'Right, then, I'll leave you with Mr Stokes, if you don't mind?'

Just as well she didn't, she ruminated as she went along to meet Mr Stokes. Going home for a midday snack appeared to be a luxury of the past. Not that she minded. She was happy to fill in – when it was appreciated. It was just that occasionally she felt that Josh was taking her for granted – or at least her availability. The absence of Angela, the practice nurse, left a gap and increasingly she found herself filling it.

In Josh's room she discovered a dear little

man. He tried to jump to his feet and almost toppled over. 'Oops,' he grinned, and sat down again with an embarrassed sigh.

'Let me help,' Daisy smiled, and went over to ease him up. Much to her dismay, he was shaking like a leaf.

'Nerves,' he mumbled apologetically, and Daisy tucked his arm through hers, bringing a smile to his face. 'Nice doctor, too,' he went on as they stumbled forward. 'He really tried to put me at my ease. Something you don't get much any more – an old-fashioned bedside manner. I've just moved to Summerforde and one of the things I dreaded was coming to a new doctor. But this one ... he's all right.'

Yes, he was, she found herself agreeing silently. Despite her initial reservations Josh handled the patients sympathetically. For a man who'd been laboratory-grounded for so long, he had done pretty well. Almost too well ... almost as though he was enjoying the work.

In the treatment room, she helped Mr Stokes to disrobe and gently eased him up onto the Incopad on the bench. 'Just tell me something about yourself and we'll get this done in no time.'

'Oh, I was a bandsman in the Guards,' he told her proudly, and while he was lost in reminiscences she was able to remove his drainage bag and let the catheter drain into the receiver virtually without him knowing. Then, rinsing her hands and slipping on fresh sterile gloves, she aspirated the catheter prior to the irrigation.

'Beautiful tuba, it was,' sighed Mr Stokes. 'The best instrument I ever played.'

Smiling and giving the odd reply, she continued the irrigation without a hitch and finally reconnected a new drainage bag. 'All done,' she smiled, and squeezed the now calm hands. 'Your catheter was blocking, that was all. You just needed your first thousand-mile service.'

He laughed incredulously. 'Is that all it was? I can't believe it's over. I was so uncomfortable. I thought I'd never get straight.'

She helped him off the bench. 'Well, while we make sure you're draining I'll give you a few hints on how to cope with the catheter until you go in for your op, if you like.'

'Oh, you treasure,' he sighed. 'I'm so glad I came here. I'm very lucky to have found such a good doctor and nurse. You make a fine team, the pair of you.'

It was Daisy's turn to look embarrassed. The only teamwork or compatibility she and Josh shared, Lord help them, was a physical electricity that wasn't generated by the electricity company – and that wasn't going to help the patients much!

It was only later in the day, when she arrived home from her afternoon calls, that she wondered vaguely how Josh had got on at the police station, but her curiosity evaporated in the face of the wonderful smells coming from the kitchen; crisply baked jacket potatoes and creamy lasagne with a dusting of curly Cheddar cheese.

'Had that photographer fellow phone today,' her uncle told her. She helped him ferry the dishes to the table and they sat down to eat. 'Wants photos of you at the carnival – all in the way of research, he says.'

She laughed. 'You don't approve of Peter Ferry, do you, Uncle Toby?'

'He strikes me he's about as interested in photos as I am in canoeing up the Amazon.'

'Well, I shouldn't put it past you.'

He looked at her soberly, eyebrows pleated. 'My ulcer,' he declared above the steaming potatoes, 'never lets me down. Plays up when I smell a rat.'

'It plays up,' Daisy snorted, 'because you abuse it.'

'Not according to Dr Cameron. There's research being done into ulcers using antibiotics. There's a nasty little bacteria causes all the trouble; it's called … helico-bacta-something-or-other.'

Daisy frowned. 'You didn't mention he'd talked to you about your ulcer.'

'No reason why I should, is there? If you must know he called in the other day on the off chance. Remembered I'd mentioned the blessed thing that night you went to the hospital. Started me on some new pills.'

She stared at him in dismay. 'Well, thank you for telling me – eventually!'

Grey brows lifted archly. 'Isn't there such a thing as the Hippocratic oath? Just because I'm in my dotage doesn't mean to say I've no privacy left. Anyway, Josh Cameron's on my wavelength. More than I can say for the other one.'

'That's not fair – you hardly know Peter!' Daisy felt her appetite vanishing. 'Heavens above, he's only asking for a few photos. You'd think he was Bluebeard himself!'

In the silence that followed she felt ashamed of her flash of temper. The fact that Josh had treated her uncle without telling her had made her angry. He could have at least, at some point, mentioned it.

'Sorry,' she mumbled across the table. 'I didn't mean to snap, Uncle Toby. If you're happy with Josh's treatment, that's all that counts.'

Her uncle smiled. 'Eat up or it'll get cold. Baked cherry pie for afters.'

When Daisy walked into the surgery the next morning Josh was leaning over the computer. There wasn't room, she noticed, to slide a piece of A4 paper in the space between Corinne's slender, miniskirted thigh and his.

'Oh, it's you,' Corinne sighed.

Josh looked up and smiled. 'Daisy, Emily's not in. I'm afraid she rang to say she has a rapidly burgeoning collection of herpes zoster and she's pretty low at the moment.'

'Shingles?' Her heart sank. 'How bad?'

'Anyone's guess, I'm afraid. Her GP's started her on acyclovir and analgesics and without a doubt she'll be off for a few weeks.'

'A few weeks?' She sighed. 'You'll be bringing in an agency temp, I suppose.'

He half turned and shrugged. 'No point. Corinne's agreed to stand in.'

Daisy's jaw dropped and she tried, too late, to close it. How could he imagine for a moment that Corinne was capable of handling Reception?

He gave her a curious frown. 'Kathleen's blood result is in this morning and it's as I thought. She needs an increase in Thyroxine. Will you be seeing her today by any chance?'

She nodded abstractedly, still in shock, barely hearing what he was saying.

'If you can't manage it, I'll find time after surgery,' he added, and began to fold the prescription back into the notes.

Daisy reached out. 'No, no, I'll take it.'

He nodded. 'Right. I'll press on... Oh, just one thing more.' Bending over the appointments diary, palms leaning heavily on the desk, he studied the book. 'Before you leave could you outline a few of the patients for Corinne – those booked for today? I think you know most of them, don't you?'

Glancing at the diary, she saw that she did. Mrs Weir had been widowed recently and probably needed a word of comfort. Alana Rice had just had twins – and Irene Davis was on the point of delivery.

But Daisy was in for a shock. When Josh disappeared into his room Corinne stretched across and deliberately closed the diary. 'I can manage perfectly. No need for you to stay,' she said calmly, and switched on her terminal.

Taking a breath, Daisy felt herself sympathising wholeheartedly with Emily. Well, if Corinne thought she could cope, fine – the patients might suffer, but what did that matter? The computer was sure to receive lots of tender loving care!

Her first call was to Kathleen Ferry.

Relieved to find her alone, she explained the increase of Thyroxine, having stopped off at the chemist's beforehand to have the prescription dispensed. Then, having managed to squeeze the Adamses in before midday, she hurried home to Uncle Toby because of her guilty conscience after last night and a sudden, raging need for an injection of energy.

Josh rang her as they were eating a chicken

and salad sandwich, watching the midday news on TV.

'Sorry about this,' he apologised wearily, 'but I'm going to visit Daniel. I know we aren't officially visiting together any more but I thought you might like to come too?'

She hesitated a moment, hearing the tiredness in his voice, and her heart tightened. 'Can you give me a quarter of an hour?'

'No problem. I'll see you there. Daisy?'

'Yes?'

'When can I–?'

'Josh, don't.'

'Whatever you say won't make any difference. I'm sill going to ask. When can I see you?'

'In fifteen minutes,' she said quickly, and thrust the phone down.

He was already there, waiting in the Mercedes, and he smiled at her as they met on the pavement and murmured, 'Thanks for coming. But you know my question wasn't about our working hours.'

'I know,' she smiled. 'Hard cheese.'

'Aagh!' he gasped, and thrust a fist at his chest. 'Cold-hearted woman. What do I have to do to get your undivided attention?'

'See Daniel for me and try to work out something.'

He grinned. 'You need a miracle, not a doctor.'

In the entrance lobby, he pressed the digits on the control panel which invited Daniel to speak on the intercom. 'No answer. A bit unusual, isn't it?'

'I don't understand. He's always in.'

After several more attempts Josh hailed the caretaker. Soon the heavy glass doors parted and all three of them were on their way to the eighth floor.

Why hadn't she come before? Why hadn't she acted more quickly? Daisy berated herself as the caretaker repeatedly pressed the flat's bell push without reply.

'He must be in,' she groaned. 'Perhaps he's asleep, or has his headphones on?'

'I think you'd better open up,' Josh decided.

A few seconds later the caretaker had let them into the flat. All the blinds were drawn and the electric lights blazed. Daisy noticed a sandwich on a coffee-table, freshly made. 'He's here,' she sighed in relief.

A relief which instantly evaporated as she glanced towards the kitchen and saw Daniel's slippered feet protruding from behind the glass door.

Josh spotted them too. 'Phone for an ambulance,' he shouted to the caretaker.

In the kitchen Josh flung out a warning arm. 'Don't go near him. It's the electric kettle and that death trap he's got attached to it. Do you see? It's a crude extension lead of some kind. I can't tell if it's live – the adaptor is still in his hand. Find the mains and switch off, will you?'

Aware of Josh delving through cupboards, she ran back into the living room. 'Mains?' she called, and the caretaker pointed to the hall.

She found the small square cupboard under an alcove straight away, and, opening it, she shot up the central lever.

Darkness fell and she fumbled her way back into the other room, managing to draw the blinds and let in daylight. In the kitchen, Josh had used a wooden broom from one of the cupboards to push the lethal flex away. Then he'd turned Daniel on his side in the recovery position, with his head tilted back and his upper arm and thigh swung out to form right angles.

'It's a miracle he's breathing,' Josh sighed as he monitored Daniel's pulse. 'It must have happened the minute before we arrived. Pulse is weak, body temperature's down... Find something to cover him, will you?'

Daisy unearthed a blanket from one of the bedrooms and as they wrapped it around the shivering limbs they heard the distant wail of a siren.

Josh glanced at her. 'That's probably for us. What about the ambulance crew? Will they be able to get in?'

Daisy got to her feet. 'I'd better go down.

The caretaker looks almost as white as Daniel.'

A slow-moving, obese man, the caretaker puffed his way to the lift with her and luckily it was already there, waiting for them – an unexpected bonus. When they arrived on the ground floor the ambulance crew had just reached the security doors and were peering in.

'Flat 122,' she told them quickly as she let them in. 'Eighth floor. Dr Cameron's in attendance. Daniel's alive but very badly shocked.'

The ascension in the tiny lift, with two burly paramedics and their equipment, was a squeeze, but Daisy used the opportunity to relay a few details and explain something of Daniel's history.

And as they arrived in the kitchen Daniel opened his eyes and was sick.

'It's all right, Daniel,' Josh said, thrusting a receptacle under his chin. 'You've had a shock. The nausea will pass.'

Then Daniel began to shiver and his breathing became shallow and rapid. 'Better get that neck brace on,' he told one of the paramedics. 'His BP's low and he's in a cold sweat, which isn't surprising, I suppose, if you've had two-forty volts pushed through you. But other than that I can't find any external problems. Maybe a bit of burning on his fingers.'

Over Josh's head Daisy mouthed, You'll be fine. Daniel gave her what she hoped was a crooked smile.

The two paramedics wove their way out of the flat, with Daniel lying quietly with his eyes closed, safely strapped to the stretcher.

'Sorry I wasn't much help,' Josh apologised when they found themselves alone.

She shrugged. 'I just feel terrible about Daniel. I knew there was something wrong but I didn't expect this.'

Josh was clearly annoyed as he hurriedly packed his case. 'Damn it, it could have been avoided if he'd bought himself a new kettle!'

Daisy sighed. 'I should have checked. It wouldn't have taken me ten minutes to buy him a new one if I'd bothered to look.'

'Hey!' He dropped his case and turned her back to face him. 'Look, I didn't mean it was your responsibility.'

She shook her head helplessly. 'But I'm his only link with the outside world. He doesn't have family or a home help or any friends.'

'You can't do everything.' He gently tilted up her chin. 'Listen, you saved the day. If you hadn't asked me to come, he wouldn't be going down in that lift right now.'

She nodded but she didn't feel much better.

'Come on, cheer up. He's going to be OK.'

'Do you think so?'

'I'm sure of it.'

She looked up into the beautiful grey eyes fringed with thick black lashes, her mouth parting on a sigh as she felt the warmth of his body, the soothing balm of his concern and tenderness. Then, before she could answer, he bent to kiss her forehead, his lips lingering on her skin as he brushed the strands of silky black hair away from her brow with gentle fingers to find a place where he could kiss again. 'Oh, Daisy. What's going on with us?'

She felt the heat of the fingers wrapped around her arms, the extraordinary sensation seeming to melt her bones underneath. 'I don't–'

'You know what I mean.' He laid two warm fingers over her mouth so that she couldn't speak. 'I want you, Daisy – oh, God, I want you.'

It was a moment when her heart seemed to stop, and she barely heard the voices in the corridor.

He sighed and let her go, gently pushing her away to a safe distance.

A mere second later a uniformed policeman arrived at the open door. 'I'm afraid I'll have to take a statement from you both,' he told them with an apologetic shrug. 'Sorry; it shouldn't take too long.'

Josh drew a hand across his chin, then thrust it up and through his dark hair, finally giving his shoulders a sharp tug back. 'Can I give you mine at the hospital, Officer? I'd like to catch up with my patient.'

The policeman nodded but raised his eyebrows at Daisy. 'Might as well take yours, miss, if you're not rushing off? Save time later.'

She managed a throaty agreement, meeting Josh's glance briefly before he disappeared.

He wanted her.

And she wanted him.

So where did that leave them?

They couldn't go on like this for ever, playing cat and mouse. The problem was that she knew what she wanted. She knew because she was in love. And love made her want the things that Josh would never want: marriage, security, children.

Her only hope, she supposed as she watched the policeman sink down into a chair, was to pray that he might eventually change his mind.

CHAPTER SIX

It was the first time Daisy had ever given a statement to the police.

Alone in Daniel's flat with the policeman, she gave a brief description of events, not the easiest of tasks after what had happened with Josh.

Finally it was over and she left the flats and climbed into her car feeling world-weary. The Mercedes was still parked beside her car. Josh must have managed to catch the ambulance and travel with Daniel.

She tried to prepare herself for the natal clinic and was relieved to find only a handful of women waiting, which meant she could do BPs and weighings before Josh arrived back. Hopefully the police wouldn't keep him too long.

They didn't. He arrived by police car a little later and she heard him call to his first patient as she was talking to Irene Davis in the treatment room, wondering if the scales were going to collapse under her enormous weight.

'That's disgusting,' Irene sighed as she limped off. 'I've put on three stone. By rights I should have triplets.'

Daisy laughed. 'No, your scan is definitely just for one. Don't worry, you'll lose it afterwards on a proper eating regime and exercise.'

Irene didn't look too convinced as she flopped onto the examination bench. 'I'm so huge I'm sure I'm well over a week past my date.'

Daisy gently felt her stomach, listening to the tiny beats and movements through the stethoscope. 'I really shouldn't worry,' she said soothingly. 'Did you know that if you're not sure of your dates you could have conceived midway through your cycle, but this could be estimated at four weeks, only two weeks after conception?'

Irene puffed. 'Sounds complicated. But yes, you mean I might just have put on more weight and feel as if I'm overdue?'

Daisy nodded. 'In all, the entire pregnancy could be said to have lasted forty weeks, not thirty-eight, but that's just one theory. Ask Dr Cameron when you see him.'

'If I can remember!' Irene blushed. 'I get a bit tongue-tied when I see him. He doesn't look like a doctor at all. So blooming glam! And here I am, like a Christmas pudding, ready to explode!'

Both women giggled and Daisy helped Irene up into a sitting position. 'You look wonderfully healthy,' she sighed. 'You make me feel envious.'

'Me?' Irene hooted. 'You need glasses.'

Daisy sighed. 'It's unfair. Women always look radiant in pregnancy.'

Irene frowned. 'Well, I don't recommend getting pregnant just to look good. My mum keeps telling me it's the twenty years after I have to worry about.'

They laughed again and Daisy realised the thought of babies had made her broody for a second. Hormones, she guessed. Every woman finally got around to thinking about babies, but the general idea was that you earmarked a father first!

After Irene left she saw the last three remaining pregnant women and tidied away the trolley, her mind stubbornly drifting back to the scene in Daniel's flat. Josh would be involved with the rest of his surgery for the next hour and while Corinne was occupied with patients ... perhaps it was best to leave. Sleep on the whole thing.

In the porch she bumped into Irene who was waiting to be collected by her husband.

'What's the verdict?' Daisy hesitated before pushing open the outer door.

Irene shook her head miserably. 'Dr Cameron says if it doesn't happen by the weekend they'll take me in. Just what I didn't want. I had a friend who was induced...'

Daisy reached out and squeezed her arm. 'Don't listen to the horror stories. Believe me, there are plenty to choose from.

123

Besides, I've a feeling you won't need to be called in.'

Irene sighed. 'Really? I wish I felt the same. Oh, look, there's Mike. Thanks, Daisy. I hope I don't see you again!'

She watched as Irene waddled out and sank like stone into the front seat of a blue Volvo estate.

As Daisy slipped into her own car and turned the key in the ignition she was lost in thought. Babies. Milky bundles of pink skin and bright, beady eyes. Crying constantly, wet and windy, but oh, so much the making of a woman. What Irene said was true, though; the first bit was easy. It was the lifetime afterwards that got harder.

Glancing into her side mirror, she was about to drive off when a face appeared at the passenger window.

She stared in surprise. 'Josh!'

'Hold on!' He tugged at the door and pulled it open. 'Where are you flying off to?'

'I'd finished–'

'Couldn't you have waited and looked in between patients?'

She flushed. 'I'm sorry … I didn't think.'

'Is it what I said?'

Her colour deepened.

He looked at her steadily. 'Look, Daisy, we need to talk. Every time I try, you shoot off somewhere or I get called away. I meant what I said.'

'Josh, this is—'

'Ridiculous talking in the middle of the street,' he finished for her, and with a deep sigh jumped in, banging his knees again.

'What about your patients?'

'They can wait for a bit.' He shuffled around in the seat uncomfortably. 'Just switch off, will you?'

She'd forgotten the engine was still running and flicked off the key. 'What about Daniel?' she asked evasively.

He shook his head. 'Daniel is OK. The burn isn't serious though they're treating him for possible concussion. He's got an egg on his head the size of a football and a sprained wrist. No internal damage. Hopefully, that'll be it.'

She sighed. 'That's a relief. I've been so worried about him and after today—'

'I wish you were as worried over me.' His lips curled into a soft smile.

She sat back in the seat and stared at her hands folded in her lap. 'I don't worry about you ... but I do think about you. About us.'

'You admit I'm right, then? We're avoiding the issue?'

She shook her head. 'Josh, this is madness!'

'Why is it madness?'

'Because it is. Because you and I – we're from different worlds, because we have so little in common, because we think differently, because–'

He reached across and drew her fingers into his. 'Irrelevant. You know that every time we look at each other sparks fly. I can't just keep ignoring it and nor can you.'

How could she tell him he was wrong?

'Josh, all I know is I'm attracted to you; I'll admit that – it's very basic, very physical…' Her voice trembled as she drew her hands away. 'I can't work it out. It's there and you're right – it keeps getting in the way. But I don't believe in giving in to something that doesn't make sense.'

'No, not giving in.' His voice was harder. 'Going with it. Finding out. Exploring. Daisy, I haven't time for hearts and flowers, that sort of thing. I wish I had. The point is, I want you. Do you want me?'

She was incredulous. 'How can you sit there and–?'

'Ask?' He shrugged. 'It's easy. You're a beautiful woman, very sexy, very bright, very lovely. I haven't the mental or physical resources for mind games, for the kind of chat-up line I suppose a woman expects. I've a lame practice to rebuild, a work schedule I would never have thought possible a few months ago and an impending disaster for Theo if I don't get my act together. But I've also got needs – a man's needs and wants and a life to try and live in between. I want you as part of that life.'

She stared at him. 'You're asking me to have an affair with you? As simple as that?'

'As honest as that.'

She swallowed. No promises of undying love. No suggestion of a relationship, just a raw, earthy need to have an affair. This wasn't part of her plan, part of her dreams ... dreams which had always told her that when she fell in love it would be... Oh, what were they, those plans and dreams? Already they were fading and all she could think of were those grey, grey eyes, that wide, full mouth, the sensations that had rushed through her body when he'd kissed her.

'Would you rather I'd pounced on you in some clumsy effort to get you into bed?'

She looked at him askance. 'According to you, you barely have time!'

He smiled mischievously. 'You're lovely when you're angry.'

'And you've got a damned cheek!'

'Perhaps I have,' he admitted with a sigh and then lifted her hand and kissed the back of it, grey eyes coming up to melt her. 'Come to the flat tonight. I promise not to drug your coffee.'

'No.'

'Yes. You know we have to talk.'

'Do I?' she asked with a doubtful frown.

He grinned in triumph. 'I'll ask Bob Gordunston to take calls.'

And so here she was, driving across Summerforde to the high street and the little square, wearing a soft green summer ankle-length frock that made her look like a willow. Her long, dark hair billowed across her shoulders and her long legs felt boneless under the smooth material.

Talk, he had said, not fooling either of them. But what he wanted and what she wanted were two different things. She couldn't ask him to feel the same. She hadn't wanted to fall in love with a man who didn't want to love back. And now she was considering having that affair, agreeing to his terms, denying what she believed in, knowing he was going away, knowing there could be nothing permanent about their relationship.

'Oh, for heaven's sake, stop it!' she told herself, shaking her head, full of resentment as she changed down into second and came around the corner of the high street.

A summer night in the square. Beautiful. She should be drinking all this in. She could see a few holidaymakers, the sun still gleaming, a golden, sepia wave of sunlight touching the Victorian houses, the crooked shops in between, with their bright little canopies and the smell of the harbour.

And the practice. 'More like a museum', her uncle had remarked once. Well, it wouldn't be for much longer, not if Josh had his way. The pall of guilt came over her again as she thought of Theo.

Somehow the car was parked. Somehow she found herself locking up, walking across the quiet road and down the narrow lane which led to the back way in.

Her heart in her mouth, she had no need to press the bell.

Josh opened the door. He was dressed in jeans and a dark blue T-shirt revealing the solid texture of his arms, muscled and hair-strewn, and he smelt of something which gave her heart an extra jolt too – that sexy, musky scent.

Daisy swallowed at the sight of him, resentment transmuting to aching desire.

'Surprise, surprise! A lovely surprise.'

Had he not really expected her? 'Ah … I wondered if you were in,' she said lamely, gesturing to the vacant parking space. 'I mean, the Mercedes is usually here…'

'I've hired a lock-up garage in the lane.' He reached out and caught hold of her, drawing her gently in. 'I've taken out a longer lease on the car while I'm here. Thought I'd better get a proper roof over its head.'

Her heart sank again.

They stood looking at one another, his fingers warm on her wrist. 'You came,' he said huskily.

She nodded, staring up at him. 'I came.'

The door swung shut behind them and she swallowed as she managed a smile. 'I can smell paint and coffee.'

He laughed. 'Indeed you can. Go on up and take a look. I've just put coffee on. Have you eaten?'

'Yes. But coffee sounds good, providing it isn't laced.'

'Would I, now?' he teased as he followed her up and suddenly she felt better, taking a deep breath as she came into the brightness.

Theo's flat above the practice was changed. The old furniture from the original post-war surgery had been stacked up here in disorderly piles in Theo's time, but Josh had stored it all away somewhere and emulsioned the walls and the sash windows were all half-open and clean, letting in the soft summer air.

'It's lovely,' she said in surprise. 'It really is.'

'When did you last see it?'

'Oh, a few months ago. When I gave your father some help with boxes of stationery. It was all brown paint and swathes of cobwebs.'

There were even dahlias and chrysanthemums in a vase standing on a pine tallboy, all stuck in as if they'd been squeezed there but, all the same, they were a nice touch. For her? she wondered.

'Thought they might cheer the place up a bit for us,' he said with self-conscious honesty. 'I'll get that coffee. Go through; make

130

yourself comfortable.'

She wandered through the bare flat. It was evidence that he wasn't going to stay longer than he had to. It was like a big, clean shell.

'You parents lived here in the early days, didn't they?' she called, trying to distract herself from the thought.

'I can remember falling down those stairs a few times, before they moved to the big house,' he shouted back from the kitchen.

She stared out of the window and felt the breeze on her cheeks. Both she and Josh had grown up within miles of one another and had never met – or had they? Perhaps in the past they had and yet with the passage of time...

'Front room?' He was suddenly beside her, a tray crammed in his hands. 'It's the only room with something to sit on – Theo's old leather settee.'

He walked ahead into the second of the two front rooms, setting the tray down on a glass coffee-table.

She sat uneasily.

'You're nervous,' he said and sat beside her. He laughed uneasily. 'To be frank with you, so am I.'

She looked at him with sudden interest. 'Why me, Josh, or am I being naïve?'

'I told you this afternoon.'

'You told me what you thought I wanted to hear so that I would come.'

He shook his head. 'No, I told you the truth. I wanted to make love to you from the first moment I saw you.'

Her mouth opened and her lovely green eyes reflected the soft shade of her dress, their expression revealing her confusion. 'This isn't me,' she tried to explain helplessly. 'I'm here but it's not the way I expected to feel.'

'Then don't demean us,' he whispered softly. 'We are here because of a mutual need. It could be wonderful.'

She looked down at her hands, folding them and unfolding them in her lap, until she sank back in the settee and watched his large body turn, pour two coffees and hand her one, his eyes suddenly coming up to her face as she took it.

She wasn't intending to demean them. She believed fervently and optimistically in life. In loving. But this wasn't loving – at least not for him.

He sat forward. 'I'm sorry, I don't want to upset you. That's the last thing I intended to do in asking you here.'

'No,' she said and smiled weakly. 'No, you're being honest.' Pressure seemed to settle around her lungs and her hands were trembling as she drank, swallowing quickly, the hot liquid burning her throat.

'I could have offered you wine or sherry.'

'I'm driving.'

They looked at one another and laughed.

'You're as lovely when you laugh as when you're annoyed with me,' he said ruefully. 'And that's pretty often.'

She looked surprised. 'How do you know when I'm annoyed with you?'

'Easy. Your emerald eyes flash like a dragon's, spitting all manner of lava.'

She laughed. 'Oh, that. You'll get used to it.'

He took her hand, nudging his fingers over her knuckles, teasing her palm. She looked down at his hands. Beautiful. Well shaped. How many women's hands had they held? How many women had he seduced like this?

Long legs, she thought. She noted the muscled thighs under the jeans, her eyes tracing the corded muscles along the thighs to his knees, which always seemed to be on collision course with something in her car.

She could picture him in Florida, running along the beaches in the sunshine, wearing just a pair of shorts, letting the sun deepen that incredible tan, honing and glossing this supple body next to her.

'Tell me your thoughts,' he said quietly.

'I can't.'

'Too private to share?'

She laughed. 'No. Too bad.'

'Then they're made for sharing.' He leaned across and kissed her, a soft, enquiring kiss, without forethought. She realised as she stared at him that they were sitting in twilight. The beautiful evening was warm and sultry and the crimson sunset sprinkled a rosy haze around the room.

'Can I ask you something?' He tilted his head and without waiting for her answer said slowly, 'Why did you come here tonight?'

It was the question she had been asking herself all evening. She felt her cheeks burn and looked away and he sighed beside her, knitting his fingers into hers. 'Pretty little fingers, but no ring. Any reason?'

'Yes, there's a reason.'

'May I know it?'

'You know it already.'

Dark eyebrows arched. 'Tell me again.'

She smiled half-heartedly. 'You're making fun of me.'

'I am not.'

She looked at him through lowered lashes. 'I thought I was in love once. I was young; we were both young. We had our lives in front of us and I thought... I thought we could have it all. Get married, have careers, a family–'

'And he didn't?'

She shook her head. 'I wanted what he didn't want.'

'Love and marriage?' he asked doubtfully.

She swallowed the hurt. 'Why not? I believe in it.'

'He obviously didn't.'

She was forced to agree. Ned Asher had been young and so had she and now she knew that she hadn't been in love anyway. But she couldn't tell Josh that.

'And your reasons?' she asked unsteadily.

'For not being married?' He shrugged. 'I've never had any yearning to settle down and I've been very happy to be that way. And...' he turned her to face him, a smile coming across the wide lips and into the deep, intimate eyes '...if I were married, I certainly wouldn't be sitting here like this, wanting very much to kiss you, hold you...'

She brought her hand up to his face. 'Don't, Josh.'

'Why not?'

She asked herself that too. Why was she here if she believed in loving, lasting relationships? He had made his views quite clear and her shoulders sagged in defeat.

His fingers tilted her chin up. 'Daisy, I want to make love to you. What's wrong with that? I know you want me too. What is so wrong with enjoying each other? We're both single and very much attracted to each other. I'm sorry I'm not your ideal, but if you let go of your dreams for a moment I could make you very happy in the time that we have.'

She bit back the tears, aching inside at the tenderness of his gaze.

'Do you want to leave?'

He picked up her hand and brought it to his lips, kissing her fingers and turning them over to run his tongue along the curve of her palm. He wrapped her to him and she moaned in feeble protest.

'I've a feeling we can't stop,' he said quietly and she knew it was true as she inhaled the scent of him, his own personal scent, her hands melting over the hard heat of his chest.

A shudder ran through her as he bent back her head and kissed her neck and the small, soft hollow at the base of it, then each eyelid, smoothing away the tell-tale wetness that formed in the corners.

'Oh, darling, I want to make you happy, not sad,' he whispered.

She swallowed. 'Then ... make me happy...'

He needed no encouragement, sliding his hands underneath her. 'Not here. Not like this. In the bedroom,' he muttered. Then he was carrying her into a room she hadn't seen in daylight but could distinguish by the soft, silvery light of the rising moon creeping over the hard edges of the bed and the dressing table.

'Sorry, no curtains,' he apologised gruffly as he laid her down. 'Do you mind?'

She shook her head as he lay beside her, his hands bringing her face towards him. He kissed her softly and whispered, 'I need you so much.'

His T-shirt somehow came off in one agile movement and she took in a breath as she saw the rough masculinity of his chest and broad shoulders in the moonlight. She lifted a wavering hand and stroked his head, sliding her fingers down over his naked back.

He held her like a child in his arms, the fragrance of his bed reassuring her, the pillows heavy with his aroma, the essence that was him.

'Let me undress you,' he coaxed, fingers moving slowly to her zip and sliding it down over her spine, loosening the sleeves to draw the top of her dress down.

'You're beautiful,' he whispered as he reached for the clip of her bra and freed her breasts, which spilled wantonly into his hands. He kissed each one, smoothing his soft tongue over the hardening pink peaks of her desire.

'What's wrong?' he asked as she stiffened, her body screaming for more but her mind alert to a certain omission. 'Josh, I haven't … that is…'

'Protection?' he whispered. 'Oh, God, I'm sorry.' He lifted himself off her, buried his head in the crook of his arm for a second, then surfaced. 'I wasn't thinking. That's what you do to me, you see; my brain collapses.' He kissed her. 'Wait a moment.'

She reached out to pull him back. It

wasn't what she had intended to say. But the moment had passed and as he slipped off the bed she hugged her arms about her, her body aching with unresolved need.

Heart pounding, she watched his shadow disappear, remembering how he'd felt, how the tiny, wiry coils of black had sprung up rebelliously against her palm as she'd slid her hands across his chest.

The room seemed to sway in the darkness; the air was heavy and potent with pleasure and apprehension. Would he mind that she was a virgin, that she hadn't managed to tell him, that he had yet to find out?

Her hands went up to her ravaged dress and covered her breasts. She had meant to tell him. Of course it was absolutely unheard-of these days, like her silly dreams of how love should be. Would she disappoint him? It was a thought too humiliating even to consider as she turned her face into the pillow.

The shrill ring of the telephone was barely audible from the hall extension. She heard him answer and then slot the receiver back in its cradle, then his soft footfall towards the bedroom.

He sat down with a sigh. In the twilight he looked like a carved statue, chiselled with a dark and forbidding beauty, like a brooding Greek god. 'That was Irene Davis's husband,' he told her. 'She's started contractions.'

She sat up, drawing her dress around her

breasts. 'But I thought Bob Gordunston was on call for you?'

'He was supposed to be. I forgot. I forgot to ask him. Can you believe it, Daisy? It's a miracle we even got as far as the bed!'

She stared up at him in disbelief.

'Oh, hell,' he cursed, rubbing his forehead with angry fingers. 'I don't know what to say. Bloody memory. Damn it.'

Suddenly, she laughed. She didn't know why she laughed – perhaps it was hysterical laughter – but it was such an absurd situation and, anyway, if she didn't laugh she would probably cry.

He stared at her, then began to laugh too, stretching out to pull her into his arms. 'Evil things, babies,' he growled, kissing her hard. 'Do you forgive me?'

She composed herself, laying her head on his chest, feeling his fingers rove into the thickness of her hair. She heard his repeated sigh.

'You'd better go,' she whispered, an answering sigh echoing in her own heart. 'This time I'll help you dress.'

And, slipping her arms through the sleeves of her frock, she bent down to scoop up his T-shirt from the floor and took what crumbs of enjoyment she could from tugging it down over his naked torso.

Daisy hugged the memory secretly to

herself: Josh hurriedly dressing, giving her a key to let herself in and out of the back door of the surgery so that she could come up whenever she liked. The way he had looked as he'd kissed her goodbye. And, underneath, her doubts. Her worries. And the little ache of resentment that it had to be like this, that she had given in.

But her first thought on Monday morning was whether Irene Davis had delivered safely. And how many more calls had broken his weekend? she wondered. She hadn't heard from him so she supposed it must have been a busy one, her mind refusing to contemplate any other alternative.

As she arrived at the surgery and overheard Corinne's conversation on the telephone, her heart sank. Bob Gordunston called to explain that he couldn't take the call rota for at least another week because he had a partner ill and another away on holiday.

Josh found her in the office trying to concentrate on some of the more disastrous notes squeezed into the over-laden carousel.

'You heard?' he asked softly, coming up behind her. 'Bob can't share the rota this week. I could try the locum service but our patients would be unfamiliar with them...'

She turned around, her heart in her mouth at the sound of his voice, aware as always of the time factor and their temporary privacy.

He reached out to touch her face. 'Sorry I didn't call. It was one hell of a weekend. And besides, I didn't know whether you might have changed your mind after Friday's catastrophe.'

She stared at him, searching his eyes, wondering if he was drumming up enough nerve to call it all off. 'Have you changed yours?' she asked hesitantly.

He raised an eyebrow. 'I asked first.'

'What do you think?'

He pulled her into his arms. 'I'll tell you what I think. I think you're beautiful.'

She laughed and felt the clamping pull of her muscles low down as she found herself leaning oh, so willingly into him, wondering how she was managing to sound coherent.

To camouflage the signs of her treacherous body, the immediate swell of her breasts against him, she pushed against his shoulders, took a breath and asked, 'And Irene?'

'A fine, healthy young son with an enormous pair of lungs, born ten minutes after I arrived. The midwife turned up as the placenta came away and she washed the baby, much to Irene's husband's disappointment – he wanted to get a bit of practice in as he plans to become a house husband when Irene goes back to work.'

She was about to ask him more when she heard sounds outside and stiffened. 'I missed you,' she managed to whisper.

He drew his hand gently away from the back of her neck. 'And I missed you.'

Corinne's voice came distinctly from Reception. 'Time's up,' he muttered, and pulled her to him in a last, swift, almost hopeless embrace.

CHAPTER SEVEN

Over a week went by and Daisy was beginning to wonder if she had imagined that she had ever lost herself in Josh's arms that night.

But on a sizzling August morning, when the sun blazed from a white-hot sky, Josh took her elbow and steered her into the treatment room away from curious eyes.

'Where have you been all week?' he growled, dumping an armful of papers on the bench, shooting the door shut with his heel and pulling her hungrily to him.

'We've been so busy...' Inane answer, she realised. How she had longed for a moment together, not believing it would ever come.

'Tonight,' he muttered. 'Bob is taking calls for me.' He brushed her dark hair away from her face. 'Don't tell me you can't make it. Please don't tell me that.'

'I can make it.'

He breathed a sigh and smiled. 'I'll take you out for a meal first...'

'I'll eat with Uncle Toby.'

'Sure?'

'Positive. What time?'

'Immediately I close the surgery door.'

They laughed and he kissed her hard until the noise of the outside world made him jerk away, thrust his hand through his hair and give her an apologetic shrug.

After he left, she smoothed her uniform back into shape with unsteady hands and tried to breathe slowly, but her heart was hammering so violently that she had to sit down for a moment, reminding herself that she had a full day ahead of her.

She shook her head hopelessly. What were they doing? Furtive kisses and embraces – thcy were like kids. It was crazy! One near night with him and she was sixteen all over again with a desperate crush ... or something quite as indefinable and ludicrous.

She managed to salvage some of her make-up, brushing on a fresh coat of lipstick and running a comb through her hair. Corinne barely noticed her as she walked past and Daisy felt an agonising sliver of jealousy on seeing the girl gaze up at Josh as he darted out from his patient to check details on the computer.

Collecting her things, she left for her calls whilst they were talking, trying to keep a sense of proportion. She resolved to stop thinking about Corinne and those huge come-hither eyes, but the resolve failed miserably and all the way to the Adamses' she agonised.

Fortunately a car parked right outside the

Adamses' front door distracted her. She tucked her car in behind the spanking new Rover, an unlikely visitor to the Adamses.

'Planning officer!' Mrs Adams conveyed with a wink when she opened the door. 'That doctor of yours certainly doesn't waste any time.' And she crammed in all the gossip, pointing to a man in a dark suit in the back garden who was gingerly opening doors and examining masonry.

'And we've got a home help,' Mr Adams told her as she checked his blood pressure. 'The wife has relented about having someone in to help. The idea of the bathroom has given her a new lease of life.' He gave a mischievous little grin. 'I'll have to be careful or she'll be trading me in for a new model – bit like what's happening up there at your surgery.'

Daisy frowned and stared up at the whiskery, secretive smile. 'Sorry?'

'You know, the new model arriving – same make, mind, as the old one – lucky for us. Know what I mean?'

The penny dropped as Daisy turned down his sleeve. 'If you mean Josh Cameron,' she said firmly enough to make it plain that the subject wasn't open to discussion, 'he's just standing in for his father. Dr Theo's on the mend. He'll be back soon enough.'

Mr Adams grunted as he fiddled with his cuff. 'I know that's the official story.' He looked up and caught Daisy's eye. 'But it would take a bit of a selfish chump to walk out on his old man like that, wouldn't you say?'

Daisy pursed her lips and got to her feet, not feeling equal to a battle with Mr Adams's mental acuity. She sighed, pushed her stethoscope into her case and snapped it shut rather harder than she'd intended. 'Right. I'd better leave you to your visitor. See you in a few days.'

Despite concerted attempts to forget Mr Adams's observation, she couldn't. The more she tried not to think about it, the more she did. A little voice kept reminding her that the man she was about to give herself to had no intention of helping Theo out any longer than was necessary, just as he hadn't lingered to help his parents after the crash. In the same way he had no more intention of putting anything into a relationship with her ... unless she grew to mean something to him, she thought hopelessly.

Completing her visits to her two diabetics and a final check on a young lad who'd had his toenail removed, she drove to the surgery in a confused state of mind. The Adamses were a success story, albeit an unlikely one. Perhaps Josh's way of doing things was the right way – for him. But it was not his practice, it was Theo's.

And that was the rub, wasn't it? she decided

miserably. Josh was transient in all their lives. By Christmas he would be just a memory, save for the fallout from his summer stay.

And she was prepared to embark on an affair which held no more promise than his commitment to the practice? Idiot!

Her train of thought went downhill after that. The worst of it was that Josh was forcing her into complicity against Theo. Another reason for taking her to bed, maybe?

And, shamefully, she hadn't the courage to speak to Theo or even Helen.

Another thought struck her as she pulled up in the square. Corinne. The girl obviously worshipped him. How involved was he? Had he won her over and sworn her to secrecy too? Not sure that she could face the answer to this question, she walked into surgery to find Corinne, unsurprisingly, in mid-harangue with a female patient.

'It really is an emergency,' Daisy overheard the woman pleading. 'The school have sent my oldest girl home. I have to have this shampoo–'

'Is she sick?' Corinne interrupted, flipping open the appointment book irritably.

'No, not really sick...'

'We've no appointments left for today; it will have to be tomorrow.'

'But it is urgent. I can't send the children back to school–'

'Five-thirty tomorrow. Name and date of

birth, please,' was the brisk and obviously final answer.

Daisy leaned across the desk and glanced at the book after the patient, a Mrs Palmer, had left. The two teatime appointments, which Emily kept aside for emergencies, were blank.

'Couldn't you have fitted the child in here?' She pointed to the vacant spaces.

'They are for emergencies only.' Corinne's blue eyes were distinctly frosty. 'The mother herself said the child wasn't sick. The kids are under her feet, I expect, that's all.'

Daisy gasped. 'But that's for a doctor to decide, no one else.'

The young woman shrugged dismissively. 'I've got her in for tomorrow so there's no problem. And I'll thank you for letting me run Reception my own way, Daisy. If Josh thought I couldn't do it he wouldn't have asked me, would he?'

The girl's open hostility silenced her for a moment, but then, remembering the urgency in the mother's voice, she tried again. 'Corinne, Mrs Palmer told you her child was sent home from school. Schools don't send children home unnecessarily. And a shampoo was mentioned – the family might have head-louse infestation.'

'Louse infestation?' Corinne paled as she repeated the words. 'What's that?'

'Head lice are spread very easily,' Daisy

explained patiently. 'They can be extremely difficult to get rid of unless you have the right application. Treatment is shampooing with special pesticidal and ovicidal shampoos which destroy the eggs hatching on the hair follicles. If one child has them, no doubt the others have and possibly the parents too.'

'Any problems?' Josh appeared from his consulting room, his brow pleated in a frown as he stared at the two pale, tense faces in front of him.

'No, none at all.' Corinne smiled uneasily. 'We were just discussing a few minor points, nothing important.'

Daisy was so shocked she couldn't speak. This was the ideal opportunity for Corinne to discuss the Palmers with him and, if need be, telephone the woman to ask her to come back in with the children, but instead Corinne turned away to discuss some quite irrelevant matter. If she herself brought up the subject it would seem as though she was interfering and she and Josh had already fallen out enough on that issue. So what alternative remained?

'I've a spot of good news,' Josh said suddenly. 'Theo is being transferred to another wing of the hospital. He's improving so quickly that they feel a change to the new ward will help him along–'

'Are you visiting him tonight?' Corinne interrupted, smoothing back her long blonde hair. 'I'll come with you if you are … I was going to take Helen last week but somehow our times got crossed.'

Daisy held her breath. Would he take her?

Unutterable relief flooded her as he shook his head. 'Not tonight, Corinne. I'll give him time to get used to his new surroundings – maybe later in the week.'

The girl turned away unhappily.

Did Josh really not see how much she was attracted to him? Or was he keeping his options open? Which, in turn, gave Daisy a knife-like twisting sensation in the pit of her stomach – almost as bad as the crushing ache she had felt when just for a split second back there she'd thought he would choose Corinne's company instead of hers.

The afternoon was an eternity in itself.

Daisy visited three of her elderly patients, including one lady with pernicious anaemia – a must for a visit. Her maintenance injections had to be repeated, the eight weeks for her Neo-Cytamen coming up. Knowing her vitamin B12 was very depleted, thus failing to produce the normal red blood cells needed, Daisy was always extremely careful to see this patient on time.

Her two diabetics were happily stabilised and Daisy called into the health centre where they were registered to complete their notes. Disappointed not to see Karen Beech, she decided to make her way back to the practice on the pretext of looking at the nurse's book for late entries.

Corinne was conspicuously absent and the front door was locked. Using her back-door key, she let her self in and leapt across to the phone, which was ringing itself silly with no one to answer it.

'This is Mrs Palmer here. I came in this morning to try to talk to the doctor, but you said my daughter couldn't be seen until tomorrow?'

Daisy hesitated, opening the appointments book with her free hand. 'Mrs Palmer, this is the district nurse speaking. I'm sorry, I didn't make your appointment this morning, but we do have a cancellation. Can you come along at five?'

'Oh, thank God. You see, it's not just Linda who's infected, it's her sister Katie and me. My husband's just had a look through our hair and he can see all these little white things ... they're horrible.'

Daisy threw caution to the wind and told her to come immediately and wait for the doctor. As she replaced the phone, Josh came in the front way clutching a paper bag from the bakery.

'Did I miss anything?' he asked with a worried frown.

'No ... I've just filled an emergency space, that's all, but she'll be coming up in a few minutes. A family with head-louse problems.'

'Revolting,' he muttered, taking out a sausage roll and lunging into it. 'Little beggars.'

She watched him decimate the pastry. 'You mean the Palmers?'

He laughed, gulping back a mouthful. 'No, the nits. They can drive you crazy. Talking of which, things are likely to be a little crazy here tonight. Corinne couldn't make it. Aerobics or something.'

She crooked an eyebrow. 'Which is a hint for help?'

He grinned, his healthy pink tongue coming out to swipe away the crumbs from the corners of his mouth. 'I thought you'd never ask.' Glancing at the door, he screwed up the paper bag and cast it into the bin, then scooped her into his arms to give her a sausagey kiss. 'I owe you,' he whispered. And she knew he meant it.

An ashen-faced Mrs Palmer and her two little girls arrived and Daisy took them along to the consulting room. Ten minutes later, when they re-emerged, Mrs Palmer pushed a prescription into Daisy's hand. 'Any good, is it ?'

Daisy skimmed her eyes over Josh's scrawl and nodded. 'Wash everyone's hair, including your husband's. Afterwards use a fine-toothed comb vigorously. In a week, do it all over again and you'll have no more problems. The chemist in the high street should still be open if you hurry.'

Mrs Palmer sighed and leant forward to whisper out of earshot of her girls. 'I'm sorry for breaking down on the phone like that. Having all these things in our hair made us feel so dirty.'

Daisy came around and knelt down in front of two silent faces lost under two mops of fawn curls. 'Mummy has got a brand-new shampoo,' she whispered. 'It's very special – a bit smelly, but that's because it ends up making you look like one of those adverts on TV – all blonde and beautiful.'

The girls giggled and Mrs Palmer, looking happier, finally led them away. Then the rush started. All manner of minor ailments and summer grizzles. It was a quarter to seven when the last patient disappeared and Daisy closed the book with a sigh of relief.

'All over,' Josh whispered, coming up behind her like a cat to slide his arms around her waist and drag her against his hipbones.

She laid her head back on his shoulder and closed her eyes. 'Josh, I haven't closed the door...'

'I'm hungry. I need sustenance and quickly,' he muttered in her ear, sliding his fingers into her hair, finding a tiny oasis of skin beneath her lobe and taunting it with the tip of his tongue.

'Convenience food is bad for you,' she sighed, a warm wave of sensation running over her.

'But, oh, so beautifully packaged.' He turned her slowly around to face him. 'Do you have to go home?'

'I have to shower and change...'

He took her face between his hands. 'Stay. Don't go. I have this feeling if you go...'

Her heart in her mouth, she hesitated.

'Can't you phone your uncle? Shower here. I'll cook you spaghetti.' He kissed her, drawing his mouth away slowly. 'Switch the line through to Bob and I'll lock up.'

So no escape route, she thought as he let her go. Did she want there to be? She picked up the phone to ring through to Bob.

No, she wanted no escape tonight.

In the bathroom, she could hear music from the hi-fi, soft and soothing and very sensuous.

Suddenly she relaxed, enjoying the warm water which slid over her skin as she stepped under the shower. The water beat down on her face and erased the day's cares and eventually when she stepped out, wrapping herself in a towel, she was tingling.

She stared at the wide green eyes looking back at her from the mirror. Would he like her afterwards? Would he want her afterwards? Was her virginity to be her downfall,

God help her?

'Room service,' Josh said through the door.

She unlatched it and a hand appeared clutching a glass of wine.

'Mmm. Lovely.' She took it, only to find the same long, brown, hair-roughened arm returning with a cereal bowl full to the brim of the fifty-seven-variety spaghetti.

'It was hard work opening the tin...'

She laughed, lowering the bowl to the vanity unit. When she turned around he was standing in the doorway.

He wore a red and white chef's apron – and very little else as far as she could see; she was mesmerised by a flicker of brown thigh which tapered down to deliciously knobbly knees.

'A little number I keep for the kitchen,' he grinned. 'Chef's special.'

She purred. 'Scrumptious.'

'The spaghetti?'

'The apron.'

His hands reached out to bring her towards him. Her hair was wet and dripped down onto her shoulders and he slid out a hand for another towel and gently massaged her scalp. 'Oh, Daisy, you're beautiful.'

She wound her arms around his neck and felt for the cords of the apron. She undid the little bow and it dropped to the ground beside the towel.

His body was incredible, like a chestnut-brown conker, all honed, with a slender arrow of dark hair smoothing up from his middle to explode over his chest, ending in the delicate hollow of his throat.

'Do you think,' she mumbled hesitantly, 'someone will ring or knock?'

'This time,' he assured her, wrapping her tightly in his arms, 'tonight is ours.'

She had a vague dread of someone climbing up a ladder to the bedroom and calling for a doctor. 'Promise?' she asked unsteadily.

He nodded. 'I promise.'

Food and wine and doubts abandoned, she found herself in the bedroom, lying beside him, the moon shimmering over her slender limbs as it lit the room, their natural, now familiar candlelight.

She brought her eyes up hesitantly. Were her breasts too small, her hips too boyish – too unfeminine now that she was unwrapped from her towel? Her legs were as long and slender as an adolescent's. Did they display any learned grace by now?

'You're perfect,' he said, without touching her. 'Absolutely perfect.'

'I can hardly see you.' She gazed through the darkness at the outline of his long body, aching to hold him.

'Don't change the subject.' He spread her arms back and trapped them on the bed. 'Has no one ever told you how perfect you are?'

She was glad he couldn't see her blush. 'You have. That's enough.'

'Do you know your name is the wrong way around? You're a rose – a delicious, fragrant English rose.'

Her heart stilled, then galloped into its beat again as he trailed his fingers down over her nakedness. Suddenly she was crushed against his chest, legs and arms entwined in frantic energy, a release at last. Her hands ran over him, adventuring, seeking and find-ing – hot places moist with desire, soft places needful of gentleness. He sought her too, taking his time after the first explosive burst of need, pacing himself, sensing her con-fusion as he stayed her trembling hands.

'We've all night,' he whispered on a half-groan and she took a breath, her throat dry with longing. She swallowed, buried in a fever of want. It was as if all her life she had waited for this. One night, one treasured, unique night…

He shattered her weak control as he kissed her, mouth brushing over the damp valley between her breasts, to ascend them and conquer their throbbing peaks with his tongue and lips. Kisses which, once trium-phant, rained on slowly down to the flat softness of her stomach and the tiny round indentation he found there.

'Oh, my sweet,' he whispered as she buried his head in her hands, closing her eyes to the joy. How much pleasure could she take before he stopped?

Then he breathed softly, steadying himself, before continuing his journey; her body was quivering, arching, dying, loving.

And then the slender threads of her control snapped. She cried out, her body throbbing with a low, swirling fire that seemed to burst like a rage into her veins.

He parted her legs, sensing her urgency, filling the need that only he could fill. Wildly and willing she moved with him, crushed by his powerful arms, as everything else ceased to exist. Her life was a mere shadow on the horizon of her want, her greed for him, the need to be one.

The pain was minimal – a fleeting, surprising pain which she thought he would not notice as she stifled her cry and opened her eyes to meet his in that crowning moment.

He whispered something, a groan lost in their passion, until at last, driven to her limit, consumed by longing, he rose with her, indulging himself in the shuddering, explosive unity of flesh.

Later, as she lay in his arms, he whispered, 'Why didn't you tell me?'

She was afraid to move. 'I did try ... does it matter?'

He laid his cheek on the top of her head, his voice muffled by her hair. 'Yes, it matters.'

Her worst fears confirmed, she buried her head in his chest. 'I'm sorry,' she whispered achingly.

He pressed her closely to his heart and, with a sigh that seemed to ripple through them both and end in hopelessness, he said softly, 'No, it is me who should be sorry.'

She awoke in his arms, remembering the careful wrapping and unwrapping of limbs with an ache of pleasure filling her every muscle and bone.

She felt the steady throb of his heart, knew he was asleep. She smelt the air as it crawled over the window-ledge and across the bed and listened to the drone of late cars, the occasional lost gull sweeping and circling somewhere over the harbour where the waters lifted and sighed against the mossy walls and composed their own sweet rhapsody.

It was after midnight when they left the bed and relegated the spaghetti to the bin.

Ravenous, together they unearthed a repast of salad, cheese, bread and fresh fruit and the remainder of the wine from the fridge.

'I should have got something special. Pretty pathetic this, isn't it?' he groaned helplessly. 'Or I should have forced you out to eat.'

She told him he wouldn't have been able

to and they laughed and she tackled a crust with all the fervour of eating steak, trying to take her mind off the brooding eyes across the table.

'Tell me about Florida,' she said – and wondered if he would. If he did, would she be hopelessly jealous?

'Florida?' He gave her a slow smile, a thoughtful, pensive smile that reached his eyes as he lifted his broad shoulders under the navy towelling robe. 'I live by the sea at a place called Daytona Beach. The house has a view over the ocean ... and a place where I can sit and relax without being overlooked by tourists. It's only ten minutes away from the research centre, pretty easy to find even when I'm on automatic pilot coming home. I have someone come in and clean and shop for me.

'It all runs pretty smoothly, really. I've a comfortable life.'

A destructive twinge clawed at her ribs. His description painted a perfect picture. She could imagine his lifestyle even though she'd never been there. A huge chasm suddenly stretched between them...

He said quietly, 'I chose the house because it reminded me in some way of here. The harbour and the Channel, not quite so blue as the ocean, but the salt in the air is the same. And the breezes. I didn't get so homesick when I found the house.'

160

'You were homesick?'

He nodded, toying with a piece of cheese and pushing it around the plate. 'Do you think homesickness strange of a grown man?'

She hesitated. 'I'm not sure. I imagined...' She shrugged, taking a breath, not knowing what she thought.

He frowned, reaching out to take her hand as she cradled her glass of wine. 'What's the matter, Daisy?'

She looked up, shaken. 'Nothing.'

'You're a wonderful woman, do you know that? I want you to know it.'

She stared at her glass. 'But?'

His fingers slid away. 'Daisy, you'll have to accept me as I am. I'm a bachelor and I've a career on the other side of the world. I can't make a commitment – if that's what you want. Not even after–'

'I wasn't trying to trick you,' she protested as her green eyes glimmered and heat flooded into her cheeks. 'I did try to ... to explain...'

'And so am I.'

Until this moment she hadn't realised just how much of a risk she had taken with her feelings, hadn't expected it to hurt so much. Was he fighting his feelings for her in the same way? Was he being like this because he was afraid of himself? She looked up and into his eyes and saw only the mirrored image of herself.

'The difference is,' she whispered in a small, soft voice, 'you haven't compromised your convictions, Josh. And I have.'

He looked stricken, as if she'd hit him. 'I'm sorry. I don't want to hurt you. You know that, don't you?'

She knew he meant it but he hadn't stopped it from happening.

And then, without a word, he drew her up and into his arms.

Their lovemaking seemed even more incredible than the first time, dispelling her doubts concerning carnal knowledge – if ever she had had them.

Now she opened her senses to the things she had been too overwhelmed to notice before: the sound of their breathing, the way he made every part of her come alive, the feel of him intimately as she cupped him with trembling hands, learning how to please him as he pleased her. She also noticed the deep creases around his eyes which deepened in pleasure as her hands sought to give him joy, and the responses of her own, newly awakened body as it willingly succumbed to every fresh nuance of their lovemaking.

Lovemaking.

She turned the word over in her mind, unable to say it, unable to phrase the words that could have so easily slipped from her lips. Love … making. For her it was.

For him?

She didn't know. She didn't understand. And at this moment she didn't care. As they found themselves in a primitive, almost violent coupling she told him silently in her heart that she loved him.

Somewhere in the early morning his dark lashes flickered and the grey luminosity of his eyes sleepily regarded first the room and then her green, watchful gaze.

He blinked again. 'How long have you been awake?'

She lied. 'Only just.' How could she admit to her hungry voyeurism whilst he'd been asleep? It had been so pleasurable, so satisfying.

'It's early. Five after five,' he said, lifting his wrist, frowning at his watch then turning to her.

She pushed her hands into his hair and threaded her legs around him.

'Do very much more of that and I won't be able to bring you breakfast in bed,' he whispered, enfolding her against his warm, hard body.

She laughed, pushing her pelvis forward wantonly. 'I don't want breakfast. I only want you.'

CHAPTER EIGHT

Josh kissed Daisy reluctantly goodbye. It was the worst part. How she ached for more time with him. Time to lie in his arms, sit and talk, walk somewhere, hold hands, but she reminded herself sternly as she drove home in the early hours that these sweet yearnings were dreams she had exchanged for reality.

She must face this. What was it Josh had said? Something about there not being time for hearts and flowers? Yes, she supposed he was right; there wasn't.

At home, bacon was being grilled.

'Sit down and eat,' her uncle told her as she walked in, giving her a mutinous scowl.

But, questions discreetly omitted, he successfully blackmailed her with a huge cooked breakfast.

After showering and changing into a fresh blue uniform, she brushed her lips against his grizzled cheek. He gave her a wink and buried his head in the newspaper.

Did he guess that she and Josh were lovers? Of course he did, she decided as she drove towards the health centre. And, moreover, he would probably have guessed that Josh was her first lover. That was the trouble with being so close. The loss of her parents, his brother and sister-in-law, united them. Even her time in Paris had brought them closer. Insults were endearments in Uncle Toby's book. And the very absence of them this morning was silent acknowledgement, she knew, of her affair with Josh.

Still trying to absorb the strange sense of new identity that their love making had given her, she bumped into Karen Beech in the health centre's office.

'You're positively glowing.' Karen grinned curiously, like a Cheshire cat. 'Is it who I think it is?' She went on with impossible exuberance, seizing Daisy's elbow and propelling her towards a neglected corner, 'I saw him in the hospital. He was pushing a wheelchair with a woman in it and a nurse called after him. There can only be one Dr Cameron, surely? I mean, apart from Theo.'

Daisy's heart sank in quiet despair. Did it show that much? Was it emblazoned across her face? 'He was probably collecting Delia,' she evaded hesitantly. 'A small, dark woman, pale and thin?'

Karen nodded. 'Who is she?'

'Delia Ferguson, a cancer patient.'

Karen's face sobered. 'Oh, I'm sorry, Daisy. I remember you telling me. I saw her once, I think, about six months ago. She's lost a lot of weight since then.'

Daisy nodded and sighed. 'Better make a move.'

Karen chuckled. 'Oh, don't worry, I'm not going to ask any more questions. But take care,' she said earnestly. 'He's a handsome devil. You're just a babe in arms when it comes to men, Daisy. Especially men who look like Josh Cameron.'

Fortunately Karen was hailed by one of the doctors at that moment and Daisy made swift work of looking up one of her diabetic patients' notes on the computer, eager to leave and not bump into her friend again.

She liked Karen. She was a sweet girl, but staunchly single-minded about men. At thirty, she was happy to be unmarried. Karen was probably right, though, she reflected almost hopelessly. Josh was so good-looking that handfuls of women must have fallen for him. Still, what could she do? Since she'd woken up in his arms this morning a tiny flame of hope had burned in her heart.

She drove rather quickly, parking ungracefully in the square. Her heart thudded at the thought of seeing him again, Karen's warning instantly evaporating the moment she spotted the Mercedes.

Once inside the surgery, only the top of Corinne's blonde head was visible, the rest of her submerged by an irascible crowd. The room seemed to be in uproar.

The queue was endless and a young man,

daunted no doubt by its length, was just about to leave. 'Marcus?' Daisy gasped in surprise. The boy stared at her, panic written in his eyes. 'Is it Mum?' she asked uncertainly.

He looked down at his feet. 'Sort of.'

She glanced along the hall, wondering if Josh was with a patient. Then an idea struck her. 'Come on,' she said quietly. 'Let's find a quiet spot.'

She could sense that he came unwillingly, every step an effort, and in the small but patientless treatment room she hauled out a couple of chairs. 'I'm sorry this is so cramped. But it's better than waiting out there. I'll try to catch Dr Cameron between patients.'

He chewed on his lip, sitting reluctantly on the edge of the chair. 'Mum's ill, isn't she?' he suddenly accused. 'Why won't anyone tell me what's going on?'

Wordlessly she sighed and sank down onto the chair beside him.

He stared at her with a look that tore at her heart. 'I was trying to communicate like Dr Cameron told me to at the police station. He said I was the only one she had to rely on and I should sit down and really try, but it always ends up in fights.'

'Dr Cameron saw you at the police station?'

The boy nodded. 'A couple of weeks ago.

I got drunk. I can't really remember what happened but they put me in the cells because I was causing a disturbance. They asked me who my doctor was and the next thing I knew Dr Cameron came to see me and got me released.'

Why hadn't Josh told her? she wondered. The only reason she could think of was that the subject was so sensitive between them. But surely he could have found some way to discuss Marcus with her?

She tried to put aside her own feelings and said gently, 'Tell me what happened, Marcus.'

Frustration filled his young face. 'We argued again. Just like the night before she got taken into hospital. It was my fault, all that – staying out and drinking, getting her all wound up. She got confused with her tablets. But I was only doing it so as she'd treat me like a grown-up and not a kid. I know there's something seriously wrong and she won't tell me.'

It was a cry from the heart now, agonising and heartfelt. The only answer was the truth but she couldn't give it. It had to be Delia. Somehow Delia had to find the courage.

Then a tap came at the door and Josh looked in. 'Marcus?' He frowned at their strained faces. 'What's up?' he asked, coming in.

Marcus sagged in his chair. 'Mum had a

169

bad day yesterday; she was in bed all day. We didn't argue, Dr Cameron. It wasn't that. She's just really sick.'

Josh nodded slowly. 'Is she in bed this morning?'

'No … she's in her dressing gown in the front room trying to pretend she's OK. But I know she's not. And I don't understand why she won't tell me what's wrong.'

'OK,' Josh said calmly. 'Tell you what, when I've finished surgery this morning you and I will have a bite to eat before we go and see her together. Meantime, I'll ring her just to see how she is.'

The boy frowned. 'I told her I was going to the jobcentre. P'raps I'd better go, see if there's anything there. That would probably cheer her up.'

'Fine,' Josh agreed, and smiled in a tight way. 'See you back here at one.'

Marcus got to his feet. 'Thanks,' he muttered and, hunching his shoulders, disappeared.

Alone with Josh, Daisy stared into his troubled grey eyes. She wanted to put her arms around him and kiss away the strain on his face. With the chaos outside in Reception and now Marcus, she guessed the extent of the pressure he was under. Suddenly their hours together seemed a long way away.

To her surprise, he reached out and, closing the door with one hand, leaned her against it with the other. 'Hello,' he whispered and, bringing his mouth down on hers, he kissed her. 'Sorry there's no time for more.'

'It's enough,' she sighed and touched his cheek. 'I can wait my turn.'

He lifted an eyebrow. 'You might have to wait a long time.'

'I know.'

He ran his fingers through her hair and then smiled resignedly. 'I'll have to talk to Delia. There's nothing I can do now but advise her to tell Marcus. You understand that, don't you?'

'Yes.' She swallowed hard. 'Will you phone her?'

'I'll do it now.'

'She's obviously worse...?'

'Worse ... and still in denial for Marcus's sake.' He frowned. 'Did you get home all right?'

'Oh, yes.' She smiled weakly. 'And I was force-fed a mountainous breakfast.' She hesitated. 'Josh, why haven't you talked to me about Uncle Toby? About treating him?'

He pushed his hands into his pockets and shrugged. 'It's a new treatment. An antibiotic to deal with stomach bacteria. In its early stages yet. Your uncle didn't want your hopes raised then possibly dashed.'

She held her breath. 'I'm a nurse, Josh. Surely you could have given me the benefit of the doubt?'

He nodded. 'I guess I didn't want to rock the boat.'

'Between us? Is that why you didn't talk to me about Delia and the overdose and Marcus and his drinking?'

He shook his head tiredly. 'I suppose so. Daisy, can we talk about this some other time?'

She stiffened, sobered by the professionalism in his tone. He smiled, though his eyes seemed to focus elsewhere, and as they parted she felt a cold loneliness freezing into her bones.

She must get used to this, she told herself sensibly. It had been wrong of her to bring up personal issues in the middle of work.

As for the bedlam outside ... well, Corinne would have to find her own way out of trouble this morning, she decided as she collected her case and checked her list, then slipped quietly out of the back door.

Feeling guilty all day for having deserted the sinking ship, Daisy ploughed through her patients. Fortunately the Adamses didn't object to her arriving late, but her elderly patient with leg ulcers had almost given up hope, and grumbled.

However, her main concern was for the second of her diabetic patients registered with the health centre. Discovering the elderly woman sweating and trembling and complaining of pins and needles in her lips, Daisy persuaded her to eat some sugar lumps before calling her doctor, recognising the onset of hypoglycaemia, a recurrent problem with this woman.

The young doctor from the health centre came swiftly, administering an injection of glucose into the arm vein and checking her thoroughly. He then rang through to the hospital and discussed an admission for further tests.

Once it was arranged and Daisy on her way again she realised that Josh's evening surgery was about to begin and his visit to Delia with Marcus would be over.

When she arrived at the surgery Corinne was embroiled – again – with one of the patients. Josh came in the back way and frowned at the raised voices.

'I booked an appointment and I expect to be seen!' the man argued as Corinne checked the diary and shook her head.

'Can I help?' Josh interrupted.

'Are you the doctor?' Without giving Josh the opportunity to reply, he went on angrily, 'I'm not down for an appointment which I booked by telephone this morning. I made it specifically for five o'clock today. I told the receptionist I wanted to be in before anyone else because I have to collect my wife at five-thirty.'

Corinne shrugged dismissively. 'You must have spoken to Daisy. It certainly wasn't me.'

Daisy went to protest, but Josh held up a hand. 'There's obviously been a misunderstanding somewhere along the line. Come in now. No harm done.'

Looking slightly mollified, the man shrugged and followed Josh along the hall and Daisy turned, astonished, to stare at Corinne. 'You know I didn't take that appointment!'

An arctic gaze froze her. 'It's your word against mine. Look at the appointment book; it's as full of your handwriting as it is of mine.'

She couldn't deny that she had taken at least half the appointments in the book, yet she would certainly have remembered such a distinct request. On the brink of losing her temper, she clamped her mouth shut with an effort.

'Where are you going?' Corinne demanded as Daisy snatched open the door.

'For some fresh, clean – and honest – air,' Daisy announced, throwing a quelling look at the girl and taking satisfaction from the utterly gratifying feeling of slamming the door behind her.

Josh rang that evening.

She was lounging on the sofa, resentfully

reading a magazine, trying to forget her miserable day.

His voice had the effect of making her forget, temporarily, the dislike she had been nursing towards Corinne. There was a moment's hesitation before he said slowly, 'I know it's late but...'

'Are you on call? Have you eaten?'

'No to both,' he sighed tiredly.

'Want some company?'

'Need you ask?'

Her heart lifted. 'Give me half an hour.'

'I'll give you all night if you'll let me.'

She left a note for her uncle who had taken a stroll to the harbour. After swapping tatty jeans for fresh ones and putting on a clean, pristine white T-shirt, she snatched a quiche from the fridge and persuaded it into a plastic container. By ten she was sitting in the kitchen of the flat, Stevie Wonder's mellow tones echoing from the hi-fi, thinking how appropriate the lyrics were – that she had indeed called to say she loved him.

She stretched across the table to smooth a crumb from the corner of his mouth with the tip of her finger. 'Messy.'

He grinned. 'Do that again.'

'What again?'

'Lean forward.'

She did. He kissed her mouth. 'What happened today?'

'With Corinne?' She leant back and

175

sighed. 'I didn't take that appointment, you know.'

'And nor did she, obviously.'

'Don't you believe me?'

He sighed. 'Of course I do.'

'Well, someone is at fault–'

'Look, let's just forget it.' He pushed away his plate. 'It's not important.'

But it was important, she thought. Why could he not bring himself to see her side of things? Why would he not involve himself? And then she knew the answer in a flash. Because believing her would mean he would have to do something about it. And doing something involved a commitment. To her or to Corinne. He was fighting her, fighting his own feelings. If only she could get under that guard...

'I saw Delia,' he told her gruffly, running a weary hand through his hair, and all she wanted to do was put her arms around him and draw him close. That was her downfall. She wasn't so skilled at fighting her feelings; in fact, she couldn't fight them at all. She loved him too much.

If only he would admit to loving her a little...

'She told Marcus,' he went on in a monotone. 'You feel so bloody inadequate ... so useless.' He dropped his head and his shoulders drooped.

She ached for him, seeing the defeat in his

176

face. 'Oh, Josh, I'm sorry.'

He shrugged. 'No one's more sorry than I am.'

Suddenly she didn't want them to talk any more and he looked up, seeming to read her thoughts as he said throatily, 'You know, you look about fifteen in those jeans.'

She came around the table and spread her fingers through his thick, dark hair, remembering how he'd looked last night as he'd lain beside her. Her hands went down to his shirt and began unfastening the buttons.

He held them still. 'Daisy?'

'Hmm?'

'She wants to see you. Go, will you?'

'Shouldn't the Macmillan team?'

'I've visits organised, but you're her friend. She needs you.' He looked up at her. 'Oh, God, woman, come here.' Then he pulled her into his lap and her aching lips were opened by the fierce onslaught of his mouth whilst his hands plundered the throbbing warmth of her body, going up to the fullness of her yearning breasts, making her gasp.

'Bed, bed ... bed,' he whispered, and in minutes they were there, hitching off one another's shirt, her hands beating his away to tug at the zip of his trousers and fold them down over strong, proud hips and hard thighs and the visible, wonderful proof of his desire for her.

'Impossible to conceal,' he groaned as her

fingers caressed him. 'Thank God we're alone…'

She gave a husky moan. 'Lie back.'

He lay back, naked, watching her – watching her remove her clothes, very slowly, for his benefit. Unfastening her coffee-coloured bra against her tawny skin made him reach out with a groan. But she ignored his eager fingers, slipping the clip slowly behind her back, letting the lace shrink unwillingly from the small, firm hills that burst out suddenly and with longing.

Gaining confidence, she eased her fingers against the waistband of her jeans, slowly disrobing, watching his hungry eyes with hunger of her own.

'What are you doing to me?' he moaned.

But he knew exactly what she was doing. He had taught her.

Meetings thereafter slipped into an unspoken pattern. Whenever Bob Gordunston could take the overnight rota or some of the weekend's work Daisy would come to the flat, their tiny, private island.

That August was the hottest in a dozen years and patients seemed to swim from the woodwork with sunburn and heat rashes and rogue viruses which kept Josh busier than ever.

Daisy made her first priority Delia, who, on Daisy's initial visit after the news had been broken to Marcus, greeted her with surprising energy at the door, her gaunt face brightening as she held out her hands.

Instinctively embracing her, Daisy felt with a pang of shock the brittle, weakening framework of the body under her fingers.

'I'll make us a pot of tea,' Delia murmured, catching her breath. 'My, you look wonderful.' She smiled and, as always, never sorry for herself, asked after Uncle Toby and Theo and Helen.

Tea was made and as they were sitting in the front room Daisy realised that Delia made a pretence of drinking, most of the liquid remaining untouched in the cup.

'I've new nurses coming to see me,' Delia told her as she sagged back on the sofa, making an enormous effort to look cheerful. 'I've learnt a lot about myself in the last few weeks.' She stared at Daisy with calm eyes. 'One thing is that I wish I had accepted the cancer earlier. Now I have I feel at peace, able to cope more.' She smiled. 'Did Dr Cameron tell you about Marcus?'

Daisy nodded. 'How are things?'

She paused, thoughtful for a moment. 'That's hard to say, to put into words, but I wonder if you'd understand if I described it as like waiting for a train to take you on a journey somewhere, not knowing if it's going to be on time or whether we'll have to sit around a bit ... but at least we know it's

179

coming and there's a destination. Does that sound ridiculous?'

'No,' Daisy said quietly.

'Last night I decided to ring my sister, Loreen, in Australia. She's coming over with her son. It will be company for Marcus.'

Daisy nodded. 'And for you.'

'I've had your support, Daisy – and Dr Cameron's. I haven't been lonely.' Delia arched her brows thoughtfully. 'How are you two coping?'

'Josh and I?' She blushed. 'Oh, difficult to say, really.'

'You like him?'

Daisy nodded. 'I like him but that doesn't prevent us from fighting.'

Delia smiled. 'He's going back to the States, isn't he – October at the latest?'

'He told you?'

'I asked.'

Daisy laughed. 'Good for you.'

'He's nice, really nice. He cares.'

'Yes, he does. In a different way from Theo. But then, I suppose, he's younger...'

'He'd make a good GP.' Delia laid her head back tiredly and closed her eyes. 'He's wasted,' she mumbled, 'on all those Bunsen burners and things...'

Daisy's heart tightened, a lump forming in her throat as she saw Delia begin to drift off, her head dropping into the pillow, her hands falling off her lap.

She tucked a blanket over her legs and helped her nestle into the couch. Quietly she perched on the edge of it and sat without talking until, finally, Delia was asleep.

Marcus had begun a part-time job and Delia had said he would be home at six, so at least they had formed a routine now and there would be someone in the house after dark.

As she let herself quietly out of the house, the band which had slowly been compressing her heart seemed to clench in a powerful spasm. No one could take away the loneliness for Delia. This was a journey she had to make alone. Josh was right. You just felt so desperately, crushingly inadequate.

As she slipped into her car she brushed away the dampness at her eyes, hoping the unexpected bout of distressing pity would quickly go. Delia wouldn't thank her for it. Delia would be horrified at pity.

Suddenly she felt more eager than ever to see Josh. To meet in their little hideaway and enjoy what they had together. The future would take care of itself. All she wanted was to hold him and love him.

A few days later Daisy walked into the surgery and found herself in a bear hug.

Peter Ferry stood in front of her, his hands coming down to her arms to give her a little shake. 'I've been looking all over the place for you! Didn't your secretary tell you?'

She stared in amazement. 'Secretary?'

'Not to worry. Listen, it's the carnival next week. Can I grab those shots I asked you for?'

At that moment Josh appeared, his gaze taking in the way Peter's hands still rested on her.

She eased herself away, blushing stupidly. 'Peter, we are terribly busy...'

'Just a couple of hours, that's all. I have to submit my work by the end of the August. I've bccn banking on you helping me out.'

Kathleen came up just then, her eyes curious as she stared at her nephew. 'Don't let this young man monopolize all your time,' she warned teasingly, tucking a prescription into her bag. 'Peter needs firm handling, you know.'

A remark that didn't escape Josh's notice, Daisy realised as he walked out of Reception, giving her a long look as he went past her to his consulting room.

By the time the Ferrys had gone, Corinne was in the process of switching off her computer.

Daisy went to her desk. 'You didn't mention Peter and the messages he left.'

'They're written in the book,' the girl said dismissively. 'Not that items of a personal nature should go in there, strictly speaking.'

'Kathleen Ferry is our patient,' Daisy

reminded her, 'and it could have had something to do with her.'

'But it didn't, did it?' Corinne snapped. 'It was obvious what he wanted.'

Daisy frowned. 'What are you hinting at, Corinne?'

The girl shrugged. 'If the cap fits...'

And before Daisy could stop her she left, disappearing into Josh's consulting room and closing the door after her.

'She's only a child,' Josh protested angrily. 'She doesn't know what she's saying.'

'She isn't a child. She's twenty-something.' Daisy stabbed the bread with a knife and wished she'd never come up to the flat for a snack.

'Twenty-one.'

'Exactly.'

'Are we going to eat or fight?' He handed her a tired lettuce. 'I can't do both at the same time.'

Daisy plucked the leaves and washed them, wishing she could keep a still tongue. It seemed traitorous to talk about Corinne behind her back but the morning had been too much. Again she had blamed Daisy for a mistake: a temporary resident, a holiday-maker, who had come into the surgery had not been signed in with the correct forms and Josh had had to do it and had been furious because he was behind time.

183

'I don't mind accepting the blame when it's my fault,' she felt forced to add, 'but in this case it wasn't.' She didn't mention all the other times, though she felt like it.

Josh walked away, tossing a reedy bunch of celery onto the kitchen table, obviously having given up on it. 'This is hopeless,' he muttered. 'I shouldn't have said anything.'

'You've a perfect right to. You're the doctor.'

'And look what happens.'

She slid the two sandwiches onto side plates and pilcd clementines into a white china bowl. Then she turned and set them on the table, somehow seeming to have lost her appetite along the way.

Josh was staring at the lane outside from the kitchen window. His profile was illuminated by the light. Square, chiselled chin and nose and that wonderful black hair. She felt ashamed for quarrelling over such a stupid thing, wasting time.

Suddenly he turned. 'Are you sure you're not just upset about the message she apparently forgot to give you the other day? The one from your friend Peter? Or am I not supposed to ask?'

Her jaw dropped. 'Of course you can ask.'

'Then his eagerness to find you was a figment of Corinne's imagination?'

'She told you that?'

He laughed shortly. 'I could see for myself.

In fact I should think everyone in the surgery did.'

She took a breath. 'Josh, that's not fair!'

He stiffened, his broad shoulders tense under the immaculate pale grey shirt. 'Oh, come on, Daisy, the guy was drooling over you.'

She froze as she stared at him, caught between laughing and dismay. 'That's silly,' she gasped, red-cheeked. 'He wants to take some photos, end of story. I wish I had never said I would. But I did and that's all there is to it.'

She couldn't believe this was happening. Over such a ridiculous thing, too.

For want of something to do, and because the silence was dreadful and the way he was looking at her was hurtful, she scooped up an orange and attacked it, twisting the smooth orange skin in her fingers without enthusiasm. It smelt lusciously of summer and reminded her of how a few evenings ago they had sat on the floor by the open window and peeled at least a dozen of them, sipping and sucking the juice from one another's fingers, laughing and finally making love.

'What does he mean to you?' he asked in a low voice and she almost dropped the fruit.

'Nothing. Absolutely nothing. Do you really have to ask?'

She discarded her handful on the table, walked towards him, and laid her hands on

185

his arms. They felt strong and familiar beneath her touch.

She stared into his face and sighed. She had to tell him. She had to let him know. That was what love had done to her. It had made her vulnerable and afraid, reinforcing her fears yet again that he was keeping her gently, but firmly, out of his heart.

'Josh, I love you,' she said simply, not knowing what else she could say. 'I love you and I wouldn't hurt you for the world.'

She saw it then, the inner battle, a flicker of remorse – or was it fear? – in his face. He brought his hands up to hold her, the deep grey eyes channelling the surprise at what she had said into the furrowed frown which slowly creased his brow. 'Oh, God, Daisy.' He sighed so deeply that she felt the expulsion of breath against her breasts. 'You know … you know I can't…'

'Or won't?' she contradicted, surprised at her tone. 'You won't give us a chance, Josh. Well, I'm not ashamed of falling in love with you. It was a risk I took and it happened. But don't accuse me of cheating because that's rubbish and you know it.'

Then she shrugged herself from his grasp, lunged for her bag and hurried out of the kitchen and down the stairs.

CHAPTER NINE

It was unfair – bitterly unfair, Daisy thought a few days later, still smarting.

How could Josh have accused her of being involved with Peter Ferry – not perhaps in so many words but by intimation – and then, when she'd told him she loved him, done no more than to remind her that they were having an affair … one which she now realised ultimately had to end?

She had tried to mask the pain and the hurt pride. It was like opening a wound to be gouged again. She had fallen in love not because she wanted to, and if he didn't love her back then she had to accept his feelings too.

They had been so distanced since that it was almost as if he was afraid to let her close, just in case she might cause him to say something he didn't mean, or didn't want to mean.

But how could he make love to her and not feel something? Underneath it all was he really fighting his feelings for her? Was that what had made him so careful to remind her that they were having an affair … just an affair?

But then even if he went back to America it didn't mean the end, she thought with a sudden flash of hope. Wasn't distance supposed to make the heart grow fonder?

A hope which somehow faded as she made her way to a visit she should have made days ago.

Emily Fields opened the front door in answer to her knock.

'Daisy! What a surprise.'

'Is it convenient? How do you feel?'

'Miserable! But come in; it's lovely to see you.'

Still in her dressing gown, her hair askew, Emily gathered a weak smile and beckoned her towards the kitchen.

'Feeling exhausted?' Daisy frowned as they took a tray of cold drinks back to the lounge.

'A bit. I know shingles is the result of the same infection that causes chickenpox but I never expected to feel this low. I'm like a wet rag.'

'The virus must have been reactivated by some kind of anxiety or stress–' Daisy stopped and blushed.

'Corinne? Oh, I'm sure not...'

Emily was too generous a soul to blame anyone, Daisy decided – and looked down quickly to burrow in her case for what she had brought.

'Calamine lotion! Just what I need.'

'It'll help soothe the pain of those blisters. Are they on the back or around your waist?'

Emily indicated the left side of her trunk. 'All down here. My doctor gave me some acyclovir which is supposed to speed up the healing, but sometimes the itching drives me crazy.'

Daisy washed her hands and smoothed on disposable gloves and a few minutes later was eliciting sighs of relief as she gently dabbed on the calamine, careful to avoid disturbing the wicked little heads of the herpes zoster virus.

'Oh, lovely!' Emily weakly pulled down her nightie. 'It's bliss not to have them itching.'

'You really need something in cotton, not a mixture like this,' Daisy said. 'Nylon draws the skin.'

'Top drawer of the chest in the bedroom,' Emily told her tiredly. 'I just couldn't be bothered with the ritual of changing this morning.'

Daisy discovered the cotton nightie, gave Emily a freshen-up and re-packed her case, glimpsing as she did so a face in one of the photos. 'That's Theo, isn't it?' She peered a little closer, narrowing her eyes. 'And Helen in her wheelchair? She does look strained.'

Emily padded up beside her. 'It was taken about the time Josh was last home. Just before you joined us, I think. I was on holiday with my sister in the north at the time and Helen managed Reception for me even though she was poorly.'

Daisy nodded thoughtfully. 'Helen's never talked about it very much...'

'No. She wouldn't, I don't think. It wasn't a very good time for anyone. There was some sort of family disruption ... oh, I can't comment as I don't really know. All I know for sure is that Josh had gone when I came back from holiday and Theo was walking around like a bear with a sore head, poor thing.'

Daisy vaguely remembered the atmosphere, though she'd been so occupied with Uncle Toby and settling in at the surgery that she hadn't given much thought to the shadowy figure of the Camerons' son. Not until much later, when, seeing how Helen and Theo struggled, she'd thought...

Emily yawned loudly and blinked.

'Oh, dear, Emily, I'm outstaying my welcome; I'll let you get some rest,' she apologized and jumped to her feet. 'Stay where you are. I'll let myself out.'

Another yawn was smothered. 'Sorry! Aren't I a misery?'

'You're entitled to be. Now get some rest. I'll look in again soon.'

She closed the door quietly and took a deep breath of fresh air out in the garden.

What hope for her was there of Josh staying longer in England if he hadn't managed to take on board any commitment to his family at that dreadful time?

She sighed inwardly as she closed the gate.

For all her loving, how would she ever find a way into his heart?

'How do you think Theo's looking?' Helen Cameron and Daisy sat in the enclosed garden outside the new wing of the hospital, shaded from the late August sunshine by a huge, striped umbrella.

Daisy hesitated before answering, glancing in through the windows at Josh and his father who occupied easy chairs in the lounge. The men had declined to sit in the garden, more interested, they said, in talking shop. 'I notice he's much more mobile,' she answered after some thought. 'And the arm is almost back to normal. He's lost some weight, which suits him... Yes, on the whole I think he looks well.'

Theo's wife nodded abstractedly, staring in at her husband and son. 'They make sure he keeps to his diet here, but heaven alone knows what I'm going to do with him when he comes home. He's already talking about going back to the surgery on a part-time basis.'

She glanced at Daisy and paused. 'Josh has asked me not to say anything about the changes at the surgery until then. Theo's deep distrust of technology has always been a stumbling point between them–' Helen stopped abruptly, flushing a little.

'Let's hope the doctors persuade Theo to have patience with his convalescence,' Daisy responded quickly, eager not to cause Helen embarrassment. 'You both need some time together. Would it be possible to take a holiday, perhaps?'

Helen smiled wryly. 'Need you ask?'

Daisy laughed. 'No, I suppose not.'

'Theo hasn't spent thirty years at the surgery without becoming convinced he's indispensable to his patients,' Helen chuckled.

And it was virtually true, Daisy reflected soberly. Many still asked for Theo and some flatly refused to see another doctor even though Josh was Theo's son – a problem which Emily would have tackled sensitively but which had floored Corinne completely over the last few weeks.

She sighed inwardly, watching the men, feeling sympathy for Helen who seemed to be trapped between the two. When the truth emerged about the changes, would Theo understand why everyone had kept silent and allowed Josh to have his own way?

Half an hour later, they strolled to the ward entrance. As the older doctor bent to kiss his wife goodbye he winked at Daisy. 'Keep an eye on them for me; you never know what they're up to,' he joked, and she felt an almost physical pang of guilt as she managed to summon a responsive smile.

At the car Josh gently lifted his mother from her wheelchair and into the Mercedes and Daisy slipped quietly into the back, keenly aware of Josh's impassive face.

'Coming in?' Helen asked when they arrived at the house.

'Better not,' Josh decided quickly. 'We've a natal clinic in half an hour. Thanks all the same, Helen.'

'Don't leave it so long next time, Daisy.' Helen smiled as she held onto Josh's broad shoulders and he eased her into the chair. When she was settled in and pointed towards the house Daisy hugged her and promised a visit soon.

Farewells said, Josh eventually slipped back into the driver's seat and flicked on the engine. 'Thanks for coming,' he muttered. 'It wasn't easy...'

'It wasn't for your mother, no.'

He shrugged, concentrating on the road. 'Helen will cope. She understands.'

'Does she?'

He did turn then. 'And what's that supposed to mean?'

Daisy met his gaze. 'She must feel torn.'

'Between Theo and me?' He shook his head. 'Helen knows progress – change – is inevitable. It's sink or swim in this day and

193

age. The practice is Theo's life. He'd fade away without it. But he can't continue with it ... in its present form.'

'But the practice ... won't be the practice,' she protested bitterly, unable to remain silent. 'Shouldn't he have the right to decide for himself?'

'Don't let's start that all over again!' He frowned at her. 'Has Helen said something?'

She bit down on her lip. 'No. It's just ... seeing Theo pricks my conscience.'

He looked away. 'It's almost as if he knows, isn't it, and keeps testing us all out? Like a little game he's playing and enjoying thoroughly by giving us all hell.'

'I wish it was. If he knew then it would make it all right. The last laugh would be on us and that would make it fair.'

His tone was softer as he said, 'Stop worrying. I'm doing what's best for both of them. Trust me.'

Trust.

Did she trust him? she wondered in a sudden rush of confusion. Were trust and love synonymous or, heaven help her, was this lust and trust? For a moment she went cold inside, then, swallowing hard, she reminded herself that she had never felt so deeply for any man. These feelings were real, so real that she felt a physical pain when she considered the fact that he did not return her love.

Was she mad to continue the relationship? She knew the score ... it wasn't as if she didn't, or he had deceived her.

'Tonight,' he said suddenly, 'we're eating out. No arguments. I've booked a table at Crofters for nine.'

She looked surprised. 'What are we celebrating?'

'Anything you like – truce, maybe?'

'I didn't know we were at war.'

His eyes were regretful as he turned his gaze from the road for a second. 'It's felt like it these last few days. A cold war, perhaps. Oh, damn, don't lets have an interrogation, let's just go out and enjoy ourselves.'

All her love for him surfaced. 'Oh, Josh, I hate arguing.'

'Me too.' He reached across and squeezed her hand. 'Listen, Bob's on call this week-end. We'll have two whole days to ourselves. Where would you like to eat tomorrow? You choose.'

She wanted to hug him. Instead she said huskily, 'In bed. With a tray on our laps. In the moonlight.'

He laughed. 'Wicked woman.'

Then he stopped the car and stared at her, jamming on the brake. 'Beautiful, sexy, gorgeous girl ... you make me...' His gaze flickered to the window behind her and a defeated, teasing grin tugged up a lopsided corner of his mouth. 'I was going to kiss you just then, before I noticed that little group of pregnant mothers just across the street pretending not to see us.'

She gave a gasp of horror, then turned and saw the group huddled outside the surgery door trying very hard not to stare at the Mercedes.

'I suppose we could give them something to gossip about...' He brushed her hand with a soft finger. 'I could lean across and give you one almighty corker.'

'You could, but you won't,' she laughed self-consciously. 'If only for the reason that you might start someone off in labour and ten to one the baby wouldn't come for another twelve hours and it would be right on our–'

'Weekend?'

'Right.'

He grinned, yanking open the door. 'Let's face the music, then.'

And Daisy scrambled out of the car after him, knowing she would only have to wait a little while to hold him in her arms ... and for a bit all her doubts were buried under the indescribable and reckless joy of knowing they would soon be together for two whole days.

It was a heaven-sent summer's evening.

The Crofters was a country house turned restaurant and health club. Threatening to take her in for a sauna and then a workout in the gym, Josh steered her through the imposing front entrance to the softly lit cocktail bar that fringed the blue waters of a swimming pool, though its patrons could hardly have been accused of swimming, just floating on the silvery blue surface, Daisy thought wryly as they passed.

In the restaurant they began their meal with consommé followed by herbed trout basted in a sauce that melted on the tongue. The house fondue afterwards was superb, and Josh ordered Irish coffees to be served in one of the lounges.

'I think we need some exercise,' he groaned a few minutes later, rubbing his blade-flat abdomen as they sipped the coffee through the warm cream.

'OK,' she laughed, imagining something very far removed from traditional exercise. 'When we get back to the flat.'

'Don't tease.'

'I'm not.'

He finished his drink and licked the cream from his lips. 'I'll have you know you're putting yourself in mortal danger.'

'Of what?'

'Of being taken home far too early.'

She put her glass down and leaned forward. 'I've discovered I like living dangerously.'

'Oh, my!' He frowned and stood up, pulling her to her feet. 'I'll remind you of that remark a little later in the evening.'

She giggled. 'Why? What are we going to do now?'

'Wouldn't you like to know!'

It was an intimate little dance-floor, couples moving over it like entwined sleepwalkers, the music from the cosy quartet drifting steamily in the air. The tunes were soft and smoochy, the tempo suited to the evening. Josh pulled Daisy close, wrapping his arms around her, his fingers stealing over the nape of her neck under her hair.

'What's this?' he asked gruffly, fingering the soft silk camisole top she had worn with a long, wrap-over skirt.

'It's new. Do you like it?'

'I like it enough to want to take it off.' He moved her closer and complained softly, 'This is a very salutary lesson in patience, you know.'

'Do you think it'll be worth the effort?'

'I'm counting on it.'

'You shouldn't count your chickens...'

He kissed her hair, mumbling, 'There's only one thing I'm counting on...'

She smiled into his chest, listening to the steady, strong beat of his heart against her ear, feeling his warmth and gentle, seductive movements as though she were being lulled into another world. Even so, she longed to whisper the words which filled her heart and which were lodged, unspoken, at the back of her throat. They would have to remain her burden of love.

The dress was no protection against marauding hands at two-thirty in the morning.

The silk slipped easily away from her body as he moved the slender straps over her skin and hooked them over her shoulders, the green silk reflecting like dark water against the pale skin of her breasts in the moonlight.

She undid his shirt buttons one by one, her hands slipping inside to the heat of his body.

'It was worth waiting for,' he mumbled, holding her head between his hands as they stood in the moonlit bedroom. 'I wanted you so much tonight.'

She put her arms around his neck, gently pushing her fingers into his hair. 'And I want you.'

He lifted her towards him. 'Oh, Daisy...' He pressed a kiss onto her cheek, slowly, sensually, moistening her skin with the tip of his tongue, teasing a passage to the lobe of her ear, nibbling with gentle teeth.

For one moment as he sighed her name the flame of hope inside her flickered. Might he say more? Might he tell her he loved her?

But then the time for words passed and he pulled her to the bed and they fell, sending pillows scattering like snow to the floor.

Fiercely, primitively, they embraced. She loved him as she had learnt, confident now in her ability to satisfy, more confident than she had dreamed possible.

Kisses rained down on her damp skin, bringing the sweet musk of maleness into her nostrils, tightening her lungs with desire, her body trapped perfectly into his.

When the urgency of their desire committed them to one long-anticipated need, he paused for only seconds as he safeguarded them both; then he entered her, driving them both, as one, to a desperate, explosive and exhaustive release.

Daisy thought of the hymn 'All Things Bright and Beautiful' as she woke. Whoever had written it had known the pleasure of waking to an English summer's day, a living, breathing organism as unique as a fingerprint.

In the distance voices echoed in the square as Josh stretched like a cat, standing by the window in shorts and very little else.

She gazed at him from where she lay, her legs curled up, sinking into the warmth of the bed.

'Let's walk to the quay,' he said, and came over and stretched out possessive arms to wrap her into them.

'Lazy,' he muttered, tickling her until she

pleaded with him to stop. 'Right, brisk walk and breakfast.' His hands tore away the sheets and she crumpled up again, surrendering under the onslaught of his kisses.

He dragged her into his arms and she smelt the freshness of his aftershave. She fumbled her way down to the top of his shorts and the excitement she had intended to cause.

'Stroll first,' he protested, but, smiling wickedly, she gave her fingers full freedom.

'In a minute,' she whispered, and thrust away the last flimsy corner of sheet covering her as she stared at him in open invitation.

'Oh, God, what are you doing?' he choked.

'You know.'

'This is blackmail.'

She smiled. 'I know.'

'Oh ... hell.'

She glanced downwards and smiled. 'No, heaven.'

The stroll never having materialised, in a state of other-worldliness Daisy answered Josh's phone whilst he was in the shower. She wore his navy towelling robe and was messily munching a spoonful of cereal, trying to eat and talk at once.

The voice surprised her. 'Uncle Toby?'

Her uncle's tone was wry. 'I've someone here who says you were supposed to meet him at the quay.'

Daisy felt the cereal sink like a stone in her stomach. She almost dropped the phone. 'Oh, no. Peter Ferry and that wretched photo shoot!'

'Forgotten, had you?'

She mumbled a reluctant, but not contrite, affirmation.

'He's been waiting down there for an hour, apparently.'

She groaned. 'Does he want to call it off?' she asked hopefully.

'Says no.'

She sighed. 'All right. I suppose you had better tell him half an hour.'

'Half an hour for what?' a deep voice asked as she lowered the phone.

She tried to explain, miserably aware that there were no excuses.

'You're not going?' he asked her disbelievingly.

'I have to. It won't take long. Just a couple of hours. Please try to understand.'

He stared at her, his mouth clamped into a tight line. 'Why can't you just tell him it's not convenient?'

She sighed and closed her eyes. 'I wish I could, but I can't. I've put him off so many times – and he's already waited an hour.'

'Daisy, this is our weekend. No one else's. I thought you realised how valuable our time together is.'

She groaned helplessly. 'I don't want to

have to go, darling, but I made the stupid promise–'

'Which you seem to be getting out of all proportion. All you have to do is cancel,' he told her coldly. 'Pick up the phone and cancel. If he wants those damned photos so badly he'll arrange another time with you.'

She couldn't believe he was putting her through this. 'Josh, that's unfair!'

'Unfair to us.'

Suddenly the situation seemed ludicrous. 'But I have to accept everything from babies being born to flu viruses preventing you from seeing me. Just this once it's happened the other way round. Josh, why can't you understand? I'll be back later. We'll still have the rest of the day.'

He stared at her, his grey eyes dark with reproach. 'How would you feel if it wasn't a flu virus or childbirth that took me away from you,' he said slowly and with emphasis, 'but another woman who wanted my time and I decided she took priority?'

Daisy went to answer and realised she couldn't.

She couldn't because it had already happened to her and she knew how wretched it felt.

She was so stiff that her back felt as if it was breaking.

Even the sea breeze hadn't managed to

put colour back in her cheeks after her quarrel with Josh.

Peter shouted, 'Brilliant!'

Not for me, she thought despairingly. I don't want to be here. I shouldn't be here. Josh was right. When time is so precious to us, why did I argue like that – and over something as futile as this is turning out to be?

Peter had been waiting for her when she'd arrived and had unceremoniously draped her over a clutch of lobster pots. Her soft, gypsy-style seesucker skirt was appropriate enough, but she felt an idiot in front of the holiday-makers. What madness had ever prompted her to agree to this? she wondered, managing to force a smile.

The camera whirred. 'Just another to your left, Daisy – this time chin up and your hand in your hair.'

She did as she was told and promptly vowed that enough was enough. Just as she was about to say so, he came over and helped her clamber through the cobweb of fishing nets.

'You're tired?' he asked and she nodded.

'I thought nursing was tiring – but this!' she groaned, relieved that at last it was over.

'Come on, I'll take you for a drink. It's six – the Skylark's just opened.' He clutched her wrist and tugged her towards the tiny inn on the edge of the quay.

'Peter, no, I can't...'

'And have you saying I didn't show my appreciation?' He hustled her towards the door. 'Just one, to bring back your energy.'

She was too miserable and too exhausted to argue. It seemed as though the fates had conspired against her, so she might as well give in and accept graciously. She would still be back at the flat by seven if she had just one drink to compensate for her half-hearted attempts.

'Martini Dry, as requested.' Peter grinned as he came back to the table where he'd squeezed her, setting down her glass and a lager for himself. 'Crowded, isn't it? The carnival lot, I suppose. They've herded all the floats together on the quay outside. Quite an atmosphere, isn't it?'

Daisy nodded, sipping her drink, wishing the minutes away. Peter drank his thirstily. 'You were wonderful, Daisy. You're a natural. Haven't you ever thought of modelling?'

'If I had,' she groaned, 'I certainly would have given up the idea now. I had no idea it was such hard work.'

'Labour of love, honey.' He slipped an arm around her waist. 'Why don't you come to see me on your next free day? I'll show you where I work. It's a mews turned studio ... you'll like it.'

'I don't think so, Peter.'

'Relax, enjoy yourself.' He pulled her

towards him to make room for more people squeezing into the tiny pews. Then to her surprise she found herself being thoroughly kissed.

She gasped for air. 'Peter, no!'

He looked surprised. 'Why not? Isn't this what today has really been about?'

She realised it was – as far as he was concerned. How could she have been such a fool?

'Come on, we're off!' a voice yelled in her ear just as she was about to shatter his illusions. A pair of hands came down and tugged her arm, dragging her out of her seat.

'My camera!' Peter yelled as it tumbled to the floor with a resounding clatter.

Daisy hesitated as she moved to help him, when it occurred to her that he really didn't deserve to be helped. Allowing herself to drift along with the crowd as Peter's head disappeared under the table, she suddenly found herself outside being hoisted up onto a float.

'All set!' someone else yelled, and she stumbled forward into the womb of a huge papier mâché castle.

'Great carnival, isn't it?' a girl giggled as they groped their way around in the pitch-blackness.

'Great,' Daisy mumbled, wondering who in the world thought up such monsters, at last finding her way into a corner of light which was, it appeared, a turret.

Still, she decided, trying to look on the positive side, she had managed to elude Peter Ferry. And the chances were that when the float came to a halt she could jump off when no one was looking.

What seemed a hot, sticky, dusty, ear-splitting lifetime later, Daisy prepared to jump down as the float came slowly to a halt near the town centre. There were so many people milling around that she was sure no one would notice her discreet little escape.

But, to her disbelief – and shock – she came face to face with Josh.

He stared up at her from the crowd and in his expression she saw an incredulity that matched her own.

He wasn't alone, either. As the float swung sharply right and disappeared into the high street Daisy shrank back into her turret, too unnerved to jump.

She'd seen quite clearly who was with him. Those baby-blue eyes were unmistakable.

She emerged from the shower cleaner, wiser and, not least, humbled by her experience.

Josh had set out supper on the table – take-away kormas from the delicatessen in the square. Wrapped in his robe, she padded into the kitchen as he spooned out the rice onto two oval steak plates.

She slipped up behind him and slid her arms around his waist. 'I'm sorry,' she mumbled contritely.

He turned, raising his arms over her head, licking apple chutney from his fingers. She curled her damp body into him.

He nodded. 'You should be.'

'I'd made a promise–'

'Which honour prevented you from breaking?'

Was there sarcasm in his tone?

She blushed. The real reason for her quick exodus from the Skylark – which she had decided to omit from her explanation – was weighing heavily on her conscience. The float business was bad enough, let alone having to explain that Peter had made a pass.

'Were you really worried about me?'

'No.' He made a face. 'Not in the least.'

'You were. Why else would you have looked for me?'

'I needed some air. I just happened to see you on that blasted float.'

She giggled. 'Ridiculous, wasn't it?'

'So was your story.'

She blushed again. 'I know it sounded–'

He put his hand over her mouth and she got a great whiff of korma and apple. 'You'll land yourself in deep water if you say any more.' He removed his hand and kissed the tip of her nose. 'I was worried – just a bit.'

She smiled in contentment.

'But don't let it go to your head.'

She laid her head back on his chest. He had never been really angry with her before and turning up to find the flat empty had been a shock. 'I was miserable when you weren't here,' she confessed quietly to the button on his shirt.

He brushed the top of her head with his lips. 'I drove Corinne home. The least I could do, I suppose, after the way she'd left her friends to help me search for you.'

Daisy bit her tongue, knowing exactly why Corinne had offered her help – and it had nothing to do with her, Daisy. Still, she could hardly protest after what had happened with Peter. 'Forgive me?' she whispered repentantly.

'There's nothing to forgive.' He tipped up her chin, eyeing her cautiously. 'Is there?'

CHAPTER TEN

Two weeks later, on a sparkling September morning, the telephone rang in the hall. Daisy had just cleared away the Saturday breakfast dishes and hurried to answer it.

'Daisy?' A hesitant voice came over the line. 'It's Helen. There's no panic but I've had a small accident and I'm on my own. I've fallen out of my chair; it up-ended somehow.'

She arrived at the Cameron house in under ten minutes. Leaving her car in the drive, she hurried around to the garden, entering by the open patio doors.

Helen lay crumpled on the floor by the sofa. 'Oh, Daisy, I'm sorry to make such a fuss. It was so stupid of me!'

Hurrying over, Daisy knelt down and gently reached out to wrap her arms around the sagging shoulders. 'Did you hit your head? Do you think you've broken anything?'

'No ... no, I don't think so.'

'Sure?'

'Just this ankle seems a bit painful. Ouch!' She winced as Daisy began to examine it.

'Sorry. It's not broken – your range of

movement is there – but it's a nasty twist. Come on, let's get you up onto the sofa. Can you manage it, do you think?'

Luckily Helen was a lightweight and Daisy soon had her up and onto the cushions. 'There … now just take a breath or two and tell me what happened.'

Helen closed her eyes, running a hand over her forehead, and when she opened them again she swallowed, trying hard to gather herself. 'I decided to water the tubs of geraniums on the patio. I know I shouldn't have – Josh sees to them as a rule – but the temptation was too much in this hot weather. I thought I'd just lean over the balustrade…' She gave a shaky laugh. 'Well, after it happened I dragged my miserable self in to the phone and managed to ring you.'

'Didn't want a "told you so" from Josh, I suppose?' Daisy grinned.

Helen seemed to relax then. 'I'd never hear the end of it, would I?'

'Well, he's going to find out. This ankle is swelling. For the time being I'll try and reduce it and clean up that grazed knee. But he'll have to know.'

In the kitchen she made tea generously laced with sugar and poured cold water into a bowl. While Helen drank the tea she sponged the ankle down though it was ballooning rapidly. A support bandage safely on, she snipped open a sterile-dressing pack and with antiseptic and gauze she cleaned and dressed the knee. Then, leaning back on her heels, she frowned towards the garden. 'Now, where's that wheelchair?'

Helen went red. 'It bolted down the patio steps like a Formula One racing car. I wouldn't be surprised if it was in next door's garden by now!'

Laughing, relieved that Helen was safe, Daisy went to rescue the chair and eventually found it lying on its side on the lawn, none the worse for its ordeal.

Helen grimaced as she pushed it in beside the sofa. 'I'm an old nuisance, aren't I?'

'I'll ignore that, Helen Cameron. Nuisance, my foot.'

Then they both realised what she had said and burst into laughter. 'At least it proves the chair's rock-solid,' Helen sighed, leaning her head back and closing her eyes. 'Thank God Corinne wasn't here either.'

Daisy frowned. 'Why?'

'Oh, it would have gone straight back to Theo and then I would have had no peace at all. She's well intentioned enough, but I have to say I'll be pleased when I can safely call this place my own again. Disabled people hate to be bossed – it irks no end sometimes – though, to be fair, I suppose the poor girl thinks she's helping.' Helen hesitated. 'Do you know she's going to America?'

Daisy took a breath as she sat down. 'No,

no, I didn't.'

Helen looked away and sighed. 'Daisy, forgive me, but I can't help feeling Josh means something to you.' She put a hand on Daisy's arm. 'Disabled people often cultivate a sixth sense to compensate for their immobility; perhaps because they have no option they use their instincts more and I seem to be no exception.'

Daisy stared at her folded hands. 'Is it that obvious?'

'Only to people who care. You've been, as I have, vexed by conflicting loyalties. Am I right?'

Daisy nodded, knowing that Helen had probably guessed her feelings long ago.

'Well, perhaps I can shed some light on the matter. You see, Josh and his father have always made assumptions about each other's lives. Theo's made it plain that he's never expected Josh to join him in practice and Josh has headed full pelt into a career of research—'

'But I thought research was Josh's chosen field,' Daisy broke in uncertainly.

Helen lifted pale eyebrows. 'Has he ever really opened up to you about his work? Or has he been so preoccupied with the practice while he's been here that he hasn't given it a thought?'

She smiled softly. 'I think Josh, like his father, would make a wonderful GP. But tell

Theo that and he hits the roof. We're standing in the way of his career, he says, or Josh has his own life to lead, as if I'm not aware of that. I think Theo's stubborn and often blind independence has a lot to do with his upbringing. His father was a GP and expected Theo to join the family practice.'

'But Theo is a born doctor!'

'Luckily yes. But it didn't stop him from resenting the fact that he was never given a choice.'

'Unlike Josh?'

Helen nodded. 'Ignoring, of course, the fact that our son might have taken to general practice like a duck to water, had he been given a little more encouragement!'

Daisy sighed. 'Poor Theo. He only wanted the best for Josh.'

'The very best. Which didn't, in Theo's opinion, include coming into the family firm.'

Daisy glanced at her sharply. 'But that's because Theo has coped against the odds as a single GP. Josh's points could be valid about bringing the practice up to date.'

'Tell me about it!' exclaimed Helen helplessly. 'They argued bitterly about updating the practice last time Josh was in England – just after our accident. Josh wanted to stay and help with a total reconstruction but his ideas were far too radical for Theo. In the end I begged Josh to go back to Florida and let us sort it out for ourselves.'

Which was precisely why Josh was making changes now, while he could, Daisy realised. Not surprisingly, he hadn't allowed anything to stand in his way this time. If only she'd known before what she knew now, she would have given him her fullest support.

The sound of approaching footsteps made both women look up, then a head peered around the patio doors, followed by a sharp intake of breath as their visitor saw Helen's ankle swathed in bandages.

'Nothing to worry about, Gwen,' Helen called. 'Come in. Daisy, my neighbour, Gwen Lomas.'

After introductions, the three of them chatted for a while, then, relieved to be able to leave Helen safely in company, Daisy left, but not before extracting a promise from Helen in front of Gwen Lomas that she would ring Josh during the afternoon and have him check the ankle.

If only she had known, Daisy thought as she sank into the driver's seat of her car. Helen's explanations revealed so much. But it was too late to say she hadn't understood … would have helped more … too late.

She flicked on the ignition and, with a heavy heart, began a slow drive home.

At nine-fifteen that evening, just when Daisy had given up all hope of hearing from

Josh, the phone shrilled.

'Sorry to ring so late...'

She breathed a sigh. 'Are you snowed under?'

'Apart from a flu epidemic, a rush on the vaccine and no suppliers to give it to us, not particularly.'

'No vaccine? The Adamses both went down this week with chest infections and one of my diabetics is poorly ... when are we likely to have it?'

'Heaven alone knows. I've just been on to the health centre but they're in the same predicament.'

'Well, we'll just have to wait. Have you seen Helen by any chance?'

'I saw her. Why on earth couldn't she leave those blasted geraniums to me?'

Daisy laughed. 'You'd probably have been tempted too, in her position.'

'Oh, closing ranks now, are we?'

'Of course. How is the ankle?'

'Reasonable. She was lucky it was only a sprain.'

'And a little dented pride.'

There was a short silence and then he said, 'I've missed you.'

'Are you alone?' she breathed, needing to hold him.

He must have felt the same for his voice deepened throatily. 'Why do you think I'm phoning?'

His mouth captured hers immediately she walked in.

With a shuddering sigh he drew her into his arms, his hands going to her blouse and smoothing it over her shoulders, then to the zip of her skirt, his lips weaving their way down to the hollow of her throat, biting and sucking with loving, intimate familiarity.

'No,' she protested weakly.

'Oh, Daisy…'

'We mustn't.' She took his face in her hands. 'You're on call.'

'That doesn't stop me from having missed you so much.'

She smiled. 'Nor I you.'

He groaned. 'But I've missed you more, obviously.'

'Appearances can be deceiving. Darling, we said we'd meet and just talk.'

He sighed as her fingers wove their way up through his hair, moving over the smooth skin of his scalp and neck, then under the open white collar of his shirt. 'I know we shouldn't, but I need you.'

Should she end this just by stepping out of his arms? If she could? she wondered.

She closed her eyes, allowing his kisses to go on. 'The phone could ring any time.'

'It probably will.'

'So we'd better–'

'So I'll cross that bridge when I come to it.'

Her breath caught in her throat as she involuntarily jerked away.

He dragged her back. 'Come here...'

And then he bent to kiss her and she gave way with hardly a shrug of protest, knowing it was useless to resist as she curled into his arms and kissed him back, wishing she had the power to change the outcome she knew was inevitable.

He led her to the bedroom and made love to her with a shudder of desperation, their needs so much more crucial to the moment under the threat of time, the phone, a knock, or a cry for attention in some other household.

She had only to put a hand over his and stay it, she thought heavily as it slid down over her hips and across the arch of her thighs, and she would bring them both back to their senses. But she wanted him too much and instead drew his fingers to the warm, moist invitation between her legs.

The phone remained, as she'd prayed it would, seductively silent, and with a shuddering sigh he eased himself between her legs, cupping her small, firm bottom in his hands.

'Daisy,' she heard him mutter, and her hand reached down to reciprocate, to draw the pleasure from him, but instead he gripped her tightly and wrapped her against him, their eyes locked in a moment which seemed to stand still.

She held her breath. Please say it. Tell me you love me, she wished above all wishes as he opened his lips, a tiny quiver going through them, his soft, smooth pink tongue coming out to moisten them in protracted indecision.

Why was he still fighting her?

Could she dare hope that he might tell her he loved her, even once, even on a whisper?

Then there were no more words, no more broken sighs as she felt him shiver against her and capture her mouth – so tenderly that she could have cried.

The phone, amazingly, didn't ring.

At least not at the height of their passion, which seemed more intense, more needy, more essential in defiance of the minutes ticking rapidly by.

When it was over, finally over, he pulled her into his arms and she ran her fingers through the slippery coils of his chest hair, her throat constricting, searching for words.

'We mustn't sleep...' she came up with foggily, and cleared her throat.

He stroked her hair and laid his cheek on her head. 'Do you want something to eat?'

'No. I just want to stay like this for a few minutes more.'

She felt his chest rise. 'For a few minutes more. Then you must go home. Get some sleep.'

'I don't think I can.'

He moved her gently. 'And I don't want you to go either. But we're breaking the rules.'

She closed her eyes. The tears edged their way through her lids, tears she couldn't explain, and dripped down onto his chest before she could rub them away.

He tilted up her chin. 'Why?' he asked hesitantly.

She bit her lip. 'It doesn't matter.'

'It does. Say what you're thinking.'

She shrugged, resentment intruding. 'I can't – you won't like it. You don't want to hear it. And besides, you never tell me what you're thinking.' She hated the complaint in her voice, the futility of wanting what she couldn't have.

He laid her back. 'Oh, Daisy,' he whispered on a deep, groaning sigh.

And she buried her face in the pillow.

At the now familiar kitchen table, dressed and tears dried, Daisy sat huddled over her mug of hot coffee.

For a moment she sympathised with Helen, knowing her agony at Theo's stubbornness and his unwillingness to change. She glanced up at his son and saw the strong features in a different light now.

He pulled out a chair and sat down. 'Better?' he asked raggedly.

She nodded. She wasn't. But she was handling it.

He drank his coffee and looked up at her, lifting a dark eyebrow. 'I understand. You've a career, a reputation, a way of life and–'

'I knew what I was doing.'

'That doesn't make it any easier for me.'

She stared at him, the air locking in her throat. 'Because you feel responsible?'

'Yes, of course I feel bloody responsible! I told you, Daisy, I didn't want to hurt you and look what's happened.'

She suddenly felt angry and she was glad because anger seemed to blot out the pain. She didn't want pity or a feeling of dutiful responsibility. She didn't want to compromise any more, to settle for less than she had always wanted before she had met him.

She wanted love.

And marriage.

And the rest of her life with one man.

This man.

'I'd better go,' she choked abruptly, and scooped back her chair to bundle the crockery into the sink.

'I'll do it later.' He took the mugs from her. 'Leave them.'

She looked up at him and for a moment the image of Corinne came into her mind and she wondered if he was trying to tell her, if he was trying to say this was the end.

'When I leave,' he said quietly, 'it will be

difficult for us both. I just don't want it to be unbearable for you.'

'Does it have to be unbearable? It doesn't have to end.'

'Daisy!' He was angry again, stabbing his fingers through his hair. 'Think. A dozen air hours away from one another? Across oceans? It just wouldn't work.'

'Other people have tried it–'

'And failed. I have to go back. And when I go it's the end. Airline tickets and logistics aren't the issue, believe me. People drift apart and forget. You'll forget eventually too.'

'Will I?' She swallowed painfully over the lump in her throat, her cheeks flaming.

Suddenly the phone did ring.

It startled them both. They stared at one another as the noise intruded into their lives again, announcing the rest of the world and a doctor's commitment to it. She watched his jaw working as he sighed and turned.

Broad shoulders sagged tiredly as she listened to him answering the phone in the hall in the deep, husky tones that re-organised themselves so professionally into workmode.

When he came back in he reached out for her and she went, achingly, into his arms. He said quietly above her head, 'It's Delia's sister. I think we must be prepared for the worst.'

'Dr Cameron, thank you for coming.'

Loreen Grant, Delia's sister, quietly led them upstairs to the bedroom. They had come to know Loreen over the past few weeks and she had proved to be an unexpected source of support, remarkable in view of the fact that Delia had concealed the seriousness of her illness for over a year.

It was as bad as Josh had feared. Delia lay in a fever, her skin yellowy, her eyes closed.

He folded back the bedclothes as Loreen watched anxiously, her soft brown eyes the only similarity to her sister's features in a tanned and healthy face. She said quietly, 'How is she? She just seemed to fall asleep and we couldn't wake her.'

Josh listened to the shallow breathing and Loreen bit her lip, murmuring softly, 'I just wish I had known sooner.'

'It was her way of coping.' Daisy kept her voice low, aware that Delia might still be able to hear.

'Can they do anything?'

Daisy drew her outside into the hall. 'Let's wait and see what Dr Cameron says. If you want to make a cup of tea meanwhile, I'll do what I can to make her comfortable and then we'll come downstairs and talk.'

Delia's lips were dry so Daisy gently swabbed them, and the corners of her eyes, with dampened cottonwool buds. Afterwards she checked the catheter, then she looked at Josh and he drew back, replacing his stethoscope in his case. 'Come outside,' he said quietly.

In the hall he closed the door behind him. 'I can speak to the registrar on duty and arrange for Delia's admission. On the other hand, I wonder how Loreen feels – Marcus too. I could arrange for a night nurse here and double up on the Macmillan visits ... for the foreseeable future...'

'How long?'

He shrugged. 'Hours – days, perhaps.' He put a hand on her shoulder. 'It's highly unlikely she'll regain consciousness. Shall we talk to the family?'

The sense of defeat, of powerlessness, was the worst, she realised. And Josh was feeling it too, his shoulders sagging as she followed him down the stairs. Before there had always been hope, even if it was only a shred. Delia was a fighter and had never given in. But now, leaving her there...

Put it in context, she reminded herself sternly. Delia wasn't in pain, mercifully. And she could have been.

Marcus met them in the lounge, pale and subdued, but he seemed to have accepted the inevitable over the last few weeks. 'If it's a question of Mum going into hospital or staying here,' he said, reading Josh's expression, 'Aunt Loreen and I both want her at home.'

Daisy glanced at Josh and saw a certain relief in his face. Then Loreen and her son, Gary, came in from the kitchen. 'We've discussed it, Dr Cameron, and we all feel that's the best thing,' she agreed unhesitatingly.

'In that case I'll see to it that you have full nursing support.' Josh made notes on the records. 'In the morning I'll arrange it. Do you think you can cope until then?'

'We'll manage, I'm sure.' Loreen gestured to the boys. 'We'll all pull together.'

Josh promised to call again first thing tomorrow, and told them to ring him immediately should an emergency arise, whatever the time of day or night.

They left then and Loreen seemed composed as she walked with them to the car. 'I just wish I had known,' she said again. 'I could have helped. Gary would have been company for Marcus and I could have–' She broke off, lifting her eyes sadly. 'At least when it happens … when the time comes … I'll be here.'

'You've nothing to reproach yourself for,' Josh said kindly. 'You're here now and that's what counts. Ring me if you want me.'

The night air had left a dew on the car windows and Josh put the wipers on for a second. Then the strong beams of his headlights picked out the familiar landmarks of the quiet streets as they passed through them.

Josh said suddenly, 'What worries me most

is what will happen to Marcus afterwards.'

Daisy was worried too, but she didn't voice her fears, tucking her sweater around her as she glimpsed by the street lighting that it was one-thirty in the morning. Suddenly she felt so tired that she barely heard Josh's next remark.

'Daisy ... what we were discussing before...'

The visit to Delia had erased all other thoughts from her mind and, knowing how draining the last hour had been for them both, she shook her head. 'Josh, I can't think at the moment. Nor, I suppose, can you. Let's both get some sleep, shall we?'

'You're OK?'

She nodded. 'Can you drop me at home? I'll pick my car up tomorrow.'

He said nothing, but she saw him take the appropriate turn to her house. The last thing she felt capable of tonight was going back to the flat and having to leave him again before morning.

No, partings were not sweet sorrow. They were soul-destroyingly painful, and until Josh left her for good she wanted to avoid as many of them at the flat as possible.

There were few bright spots in the week that followed, a week full of flu and coughs and colds and a phone that never stopped ringing.

227

Josh walked about like a shadow, barely getting any sleep, and tried not to bark at everyone, though from the lines driving down his cheeks Daisy could see that he was exhausted. He visited Delia daily and Daisy called in too. But there was little change in the situation and she seemed to go deeper into a heavy, fevered sleep.

On Thursday she read in the nurse's book that Daniel Downey had phoned and asked for a visit. She had seen him once since the accident with the kettle and that was only for a brief few minutes before a social worker had arrived. The burn had healed so she really had no excuse to visit, not until Corinne's abbreviated message to call appeared in the book.

As the lift doors parted on the ground floor of the seafront flats, Daisy almost bumped into the occupant.

Her mouth fell open in surprise. 'Daniel?' He looked so different that she hardly recognised him. Clean, short hair, a sweatshirt and joggers and, most unique of all, a smile. 'Daniel ... you look great!'

He grinned and, to her further surprise, allowed the lift to go on its way.

'You're going out?'

He nodded. 'Just to the seafront. Can you come with me for a few minutes?'

She stared at him in astonishment. 'Are you sure?'

'Absolutely. I've been wanting to talk to you. You couldn't have come at a better time.'

Completely taken aback, Daisy took a while to convince herself that she was actually walking with Daniel Downey, depressive and agoraphobic, to the cliffs on a glorious September day.

He began to tell her as they walked about how his life had changed since his admission to hospital. 'As I didn't have anything else to do,' he explained, 'I listened to Dr Cameron's tapes. The narrator, a female doctor, touched on everything I felt and thought – my fears and phobias, my sweating and confusion ... and more.

'She explained about the nervous system – how one part directs the movement of limbs through the brain and spinal cord and the other part the internal organs, which are directed by a delicate network of fibres lying on either side of the backbone. It's this, my involuntary nervous system, which prepares me for fight or flight.' He grinned at her as they stopped to sit on a bench. 'Am I boring you?'

'No, Daniel. I'm just surprised.'

'So was I. You see, it's all to do with the pattern of fear ... fear is what immobilised me when I failed my degree. My fear increased with a bereavement and resulted in phobias and accidents.'

'But why do you think the tape in particular helped so much?'

Daniel hesitated for a moment. 'Because she said something that I realised was true – that the panic and the fear couldn't kill me. I'd discovered that. I was still alive. I couldn't die from a panic attack, only from the accidents associated with them – like my burn and the electric shock.'

Daisy nodded thoughtfully. 'Sometimes, though, even if we are aware of what's going on, it's very hard to find a way to change it.'

'Which is why,' Daniel went on excitedly, 'I began, as she suggested, to make a small journey each day. I tackled the hospital corridor first. It was hard but it worked. Each day I got further. X-ray, the theatres, Casualty and Physio and finally all the way down to the main entrance. And when I came home I just carried on. This bench is the furthest I've got, but out there–' he waved his hand to the horizon '–is the whole world. And some day I mean to see it.'

'Daniel, that's wonderful.' Daisy held her breath. It was always so exciting when patients helped themselves in a way that demanded a lot of perseverance and courage, and she was particularly delighted that Daniel had done it.

'I still get the sweating and the hyperventilation sometimes,' he admitted with a frown. 'But then I remind myself that they are caused by my adrenal glands. They flood adrenalin into the bloodstream and this enhances the action of the sympathetic nerves. Now I know the reality and that I shan't be a terminal case unless I electrocute myself again it doesn't seem so frightening.'

He laughed, as if not taking himself too seriously. 'I'm doing what they call "breaking the cycle of fear-adrenalin-fear". I just face it now and say, Come on, do your worst.'

'It takes courage, Daniel.'

He shook his head. 'I was lucky. The tape made sense to me. I had one of those moments of rare clarity and followed it.'

She understood. Fear could wreck a person's life – twist it, distort relationships, wreak havoc.

But Daniel was overcoming his fear. She hadn't thought he would bother to play those tapes; nor had she thought that the Adamses would agree to have their house modernised – or that Marcus would level out in the way he had – yet Josh had believed in all of them.

Therefore, why hadn't she believed in him when he had only done what he thought was best for the practice?

If she had, it might have made a world of difference to their relationship. If she had trusted him he might have been able to love her.

CHAPTER ELEVEN

Daisy wound up her talk with a newly pregnant woman, their conversation having centred on the future but strangely not on the baby, only the avoidance of one.

Theresa James had five youngsters already. She was a woman with a deeply religious conviction and the rhythm method had brought forth three of her brood. Because of this latest pregnancy, Josh had talked to her about contraception after the baby.

A sensitive area, Daisy realised. When Theresa had broached the subject with her during her antenatal check, she had really been forced to confront her own feelings on the subject. Josh had never suggested the Pill but had merely taken appropriate steps himself.

She thought she understood why. It was one responsibility he felt he should shoulder; after all, asking her to consider the Pill would have had overtones of commitment. And that was what he didn't want.

Sobered by their conversation, she saw Theresa out, making an appointment for her on the way for October. The hurtful personal fears in her mind surfaced again – the

233

ones she always pushed back, too afraid to confront. October. A week away.

She hardly saw Corinne as she passed her in the hall, but when the phone rang in Reception and the blonde girl answered it she stopped, suddenly aware that Corinne was calling after her.

'Someone called Loreen.'

'Josh or me?'

'Either will do.' And the girl thrust the phone at her.

Daisy took it. 'Loreen?'

There was a pause and then a choked whisper. 'Can you come?'

'Of course.' She looked up and saw Josh, who was seeing off his last patient. Their eyes met and she mouthed, Delia. He nodded and Daisy said gently, 'We'll be with you in just a few minutes.'

It was, literally, only minutes before they reached Delia's house and found the front door ajar. Marcus stood there waiting for them, blotchy-skinned and red-eyed. As they walked into the hall, Loreen came down the stairs, just stood for a few seconds, then shook her head.

It was a very peaceful passing.

Delia slipped away with her family around her. She hadn't regained consciousness but neither had she suffered in the final week, a fact for which Daisy was eternally grateful.

Her funeral, a week later, was held in the Summerforde church at which Delia had once worshipped. The service was short and sensitively taken by the local vicar, and the coffin was laden with early October flowers. Friends and family filled the pews and Marcus stood bravely at the front with Gary and Loreen. 'Give me Joy in my Heart', Delia's favourite hymn, echoed with melancholy poignance as finally they said a last goodbye.

Daisy watched as the procession passed by, aware of Josh beside her dressed formally in a dark suit and tie, his presence a comfort. He gripped her hand. 'Are you all right?'

She nodded as the last mourner left the church and they sat down for a few seconds on the pew together. It was a moment she needed and he slipped his arm around her, squeezing her shoulder under the black jacket of her suit.

'Better make a move,' he said quietly and she nodded, keeping her face averted. 'Do you want to go with the family to the crematorium?'

She shook her head as they walked out. 'No, I think they would prefer to be left alone.'

'Did Marcus tell you? He's going back to Australia with Loreen and Gary,' Josh said as they reached the sunlit porch.

She watched Marcus and Gary climb into the limousines and took the opportunity to blow her nose. 'Yes, that's wonderful, isn't it?'

They began to walk in silence to the Mercedes, parked at the rear of the church. This, perhaps, would be the right time to tell him, she thought, for if she didn't tell him now she might never have the strength again.

'Josh–'

'Marcus will be OK,' he interrupted gently. 'A new start, a fresh outlook, away from the memories.'

'Josh, it's not about Marcus.'

He turned and stared down at her, his grey eyes so beautiful, so much a part of her life that she wanted to reach up, put her arms around him, love him, not wound him or hurt him, though what she was about to say, of course, would probably come as a relief.

'And I've something to tell you,' he forestalled her. 'Helen rang me this morning before I left. Theo's home tomorrow.'

Her first thought was that finally the waiting was at an end. Then came the pain and shock, reinforcing the necessity of what she had to do.

How could she stay on at the practice after he'd gone? Walk in every day and look up at those stairs that led to the place which had been their very own world and know they would never be there together again?

No, she had known it would be impossible. And when the letter had come last
week it had seemed the only obvious way
out.

The grief of the day, for Delia, for herself,
for her own selfishly aching heart, suddenly
surfaced and the tears fell in spite of her
efforts to staunch them with a damp tissue.

He pulled out a crisp white handkerchief
from his breast pocket and dabbed at her
face softly. 'Oh, Daisy, darling, don't cry.'

She managed a wobbly smile and, pushing
him away, lifted the handkerchief like a
ridiculous warning flag in front of her.

'Don't ... please. Not before I say what I
have to. Knowing Theo is home and – and
he's improving,' she went on brokenly,
dragging out the words, 'makes telling you
easier. Josh, I'm leaving the district nursing
team. I've talked it over with my direct
superior but I haven't told anyone, just you.'

In the stunned silence that followed she
wondered if she'd made herself clear or if it
had just been a confused babble of words.
His face was set, registering no emotion, not
a flicker or a bat of an eyelid, and for a
moment all she could hear was the pounding
of her heart.

'Why? Is it because of us?' he asked
eventually.

'I ... I need a fresh start,' she said and
looked away. 'And one happened to come

through the letterbox last week. The Marie Claire wrote, explaining they need a staff nurse, bilingual preferably, and asking if I was by any chance interested.'

'Why didn't you tell me?'

She shrugged, evasive now as she stared back at him. 'With Delia ... and the flu virus, we just didn't seem to have time–'

'We've had time to sleep together.'

The arrow of pain that went through her made her gasp. 'Don't, Josh. There was no point in telling you. I've made my decision.'

She wanted to ask whether it would have made any difference if she'd told him. Would he have asked her not to leave, told her he loved her and wanted to share his life with her? It would have been a pointless exercise, though, for she knew the answer.

Still she hesitated, wanting to reassure herself with the solid warmth of his body which was, in effect, just self-inflicted torture.

How easy it would be to sink into his arms, bury her head in his chest, be persuaded to stay on at the practice until the very last minute he was there.

How easy and how futile.

'Have you told Theo?' he ground out.

'No, I told you, not yet.'

'And you're sure ... I mean really sure?'

No, she wasn't. She wasn't certain of anything except her love for him and that was the last thing he wanted to hear.

'Yes,' she answered unsteadily, easing away. 'I'm sure.' He reached out to touch her. 'I have to go now. I'll walk, thanks.'

'Don't go, Daisy...'

She looked at him in surprise. What more was there to say? Her legs were suddenly weak and shaking and she knew that if she didn't go now she wouldn't be able to do this again, ever. He would never admit to loving her. Somehow she just had to find a way of coping. Time, she hoped. And the Marie Claire.

'At least let me drive you?'

She gave a hollow little laugh. 'This is where we came in, isn't it?'

Managing a crooked, brave smile, she turned away and headed for the bank of trees and the lane which skirted the church-yard and the quiet heart of the wood where she would be able to cry in peace.

She had to tell Theo.

She was dreading it. But it had to be done. She just prayed that he wouldn't ask for too many reasons – and if he did, well, she'd have to cross that bridge when she came to it.

Meeting Karen Beech at the Summer-forde surgery finally helped her resolve.

'I hear on the grapevine that Dr Theo is home?' Karen murmured with a puzzled expression as they talked in the office.

'Home two days now.' Daisy chewed at her lip. She and Josh had hardly spoken. He hadn't been overtly cold, but the calls which had mounted up for the flu outbreak had given him a good excuse to avoid her.

Was it the end? she wondered. Well, if it was – and she was still smarting over their conversation in the churchyard – she had the consolation of knowing she'd stamped the expiry date on their affair herself. A bitter prize, she decided, and one not worth winning.

'I heard...' Karen stopped, her face reddening as she gave another puzzled frown. 'I might as well say it – I heard Theo has a partner in the offing.'

Daisy couldn't contain her surprise, her green eyes flying wide open. 'A partner? But that means – Karen, where did you hear this?'

'From one of my patients, a Gwen Lomas. She's just home from an appendix op. She's a neighbour of the Camerons.'

Gwen ... Gwen! Of course ... the woman who had called round after Helen's fall, Daisy realised.

Karen frowned. 'You've told Theo about the Marie Claire?'

'No ... not yet.'

'I think you'd better.' Karen looked suitably disgusted. 'He'll be wanting a replacement DN.'

Her conscience pricking, that evening Daisy rang and spoke to Theo who told her he was on his own for an hour while Helen was visiting a friend.

Just an hour. All the time she needed, she thought, driving a little too fast through the chilly October evening to the Camerons'.

When she arrived she saw that Theo was in good shape. He was trim and he'd lost the puffiness that had bloated his face prior to the heart attack.

He even produced a glass of sherry and a wedge of Helen's fruit cake. 'I was wondering when you'd call,' he told her mysteriously as she settled in a comfortable wing chair by the open fire. 'How's your uncle?' he asked with a curious gleam in his eye.

'Better,' she said, wondering if Theo knew about his treatment with Josh. 'The antibiotic seems to have suited him,' she added. She was beginning to think that Josh had a kind of Midas touch in medicine. Even Uncle Toby's ulcer seemed to be responding, a fact that was hurled regularly home by its owner these days. She paused but Theo gave nothing away.

How much did he know? she wondered, and, sensing his eyes on her, she sipped the sherry, hoping for a little Dutch courage. After several false starts she began to tell Theo of the offer and her acceptance of the Marie Claire job.

'End of the month?' he muttered. 'So you won't be staying to meet my new partner?'

Her heart raced. Now what should she say? But all he did was laugh and she stared at him, surprised at the mischievous, almost wicked gleam in his eyes. 'Daisy, I've done a lot of thinking,' he told her gently, 'and I realise in the past I might have been an old fool, but I had a warning and this time I've taken it seriously. And I've also done a bit of planning. I thought if everyone else was I might as well too!'

'Do you mean you knew about what was happening at the practice?' she gasped in surprise.

'Yes, I knew.'

Her mouth fell open. 'Does Josh know you knew?'

To her complete astonishment, he gave her a wink. 'Well, now, that would be telling, wouldn't it?' He leaned across to the coffee-table and stole a thick wedge of fruit cake. 'The mice will play whilst the cat's away,' he added, munching. 'And I can tell Helen you loved her fruit cake.'

She hadn't made any sense at all of what Theo had said. Was it a confusion problem? she wondered as she drove to work on Friday. Had he fully recovered yet? Perhaps the excitement of coming home…

Her thoughts turned to the surgery as she

pulled on the brake and parked in the square. She would miss it. Oh, God, she would. And the flat above. Their island.

Rummaging for a tissue, she gave her nose a good blow. She'd shed enough tears, at least in public. She'd see the next two weeks out and at least try to end their affair with... She sighed; there was no word. Heartache was the only one she could think of, deep and unremitting and only bearable if she left Summerforde. Even Uncle Toby had seemed to understand when she'd told him last night. Perhaps he too would be pleased to have his independence back again.

The surgery door stood propped open in the surprisingly mild weather. Like the old days, Daisy thought nostalgically. Any excuse for a breath of fresh air and Emily or Theo would wedge it back, allowing a fresh gust to blow through and brace everyone, including the patients. Especially the patients.

Preparing herself to face Corinne, she walked in, saw no one at Reception, and gazed around in surprise at the waiting room.

It was deserted. Then a small, neat, dark woman came along the hall and Daisy's jaw dropped open. 'Emily! What are you doing here?'

'I work here, remember?' Emily laughed, hurrying forward to give her a hug.

'But I didn't think–'

'Didn't think I'd make it back?'

'Well … not exactly… There've been so many changes.'

'Hmm. Apparently.' She grimaced at the computer and the fax machine and the sophisticated mini-switchboard.

Daisy scanned Emily's face. 'How do you feel?'

'Never better.'

'I just can't believe it!' Daisy frowned at the empty desk. 'Where's Corinne?'

'Ah … long story.' Emily raised her neat little eyebrows. 'Perhaps you'd better pop along and meet the new partner.'

'The new partner? Already? But surely–?'

'He's nice. You'll like him.'

Blood rushed to her head and, trying to drag it back into the rest of her body where it belonged, she stared along the deserted hallway.

'Talk to you later,' Emily grinned, giving her a little push.

She walked on water to Theo's door. This wasn't what she had expected. She wasn't prepared…

'Come in!'

She pushed it, heart driving like a generator.

'Come in, Daisy.'

The new partner's eyes darkened, ignited, burnt as he stared at her, the smile spreading across his face with slow, cherishing enjoyment of her shock as he walked from behind Theo's old desk across the oriental carpet and pulled her into his arms. 'Is that all you've got to say for yourself?' he growled as she stared dumbly at him in shock. 'Cat got your tongue?' Then he bent to bury his face in her hair before he kissed her.

'Not a very warm welcome for the new partner, Sister Daisy Rose,' he murmured.

'Josh?' She shook her head, repeating his name again disbelievingly. 'Emily said–'

'Silly girl,' he reproached her tenderly. 'Who else but me?'

'But you're going back to Florida!'

He laughed. 'Then I'm going to have a very tight schedule taking surgery here as well. Though possibly commuting by Concorde...?'

She pushed him away from her. 'Don't joke, Josh. It hurts too much.'

'It's no joke. The only reason I shall be going back to Florida is to sell the house and tie up a few loose ends at work.' He took her into his arms, caressing her rigid shoulders, his hands breathing back life into her body, kissing her hot, confused cheeks and her startled mouth. 'Don't you know why? Do you really imagine I could leave you?'

'But ... you can't give up everything because of ... because of us. I couldn't bear it. I couldn't let you. Eventually you'd hate me for it.'

He scowled, black eyebrows knit in a frown as he took her head between his hands. 'I didn't realise until that day in the churchyard – and then it all suddenly crystallised. I couldn't fight what I was really feeling any more. I didn't want a future without you and when you told me you were leaving for Paris I saw what was happening – that it wasn't hypothetical any more, that I was really losing you.'

Then the tears really fell, cascading, incredulous tears. Tears of happiness. Tears of joy.

'You need some counselling,' he whispered as he hugged her to him. 'And I know just the person to give it to you.'

Their mouths locked in a tumult of longing, his hands finding her breasts, her rib cage and the gentle swell of her hips. She wondered in a moment of lucidity if he knew how much she really loved him. Wondered if he ever would. Then decided that for the rest of her life she would show him.

'I love you, Daisy,' he whispered as with tender hands he lifted himself from her and sighed, lying beside her, stretching the length of his long body on the bed to admire her naked, brazen, slender limbs in the glowing aftermath of their love making.

'And I love you.' Oh, precious, beautiful words. 'I love you so,' she breathed again rapturously, turning on her side and staring into the greyest eyes she had ever seen, her heart so full that she could hardly speak.

His leg was flung across her, heavy, delicious, a forest of tiny, crinkly spokes of black hair rubbing into her thighs and calves. 'I've something else to tell you...'

'Will I like it?' She lifted drowsy eyes.

'Hmm.'

'Is that a yes or a no?'

He slid his hand through her dark hair. 'It's just a hmm.'

Green eyes opened a fraction wider. 'You're procrastinating.'

He sighed. 'I rang the Marie Claire.'

'You what?' She tried to sit up, but he pulled her down.

'They were very sympathetic.'

'To what?'

'To our engagement.'

She stared at him, wild-eyed.

'Well, we shall be when we've time to find a ring.'

She didn't know whether to laugh or cry. Instead she kissed him, pulling down his dark head, surrendering her lips, surrendering her soul.

'I don't want to let you go,' he groaned.

'Then don't.'

He didn't answer, not in words, but paid homage to her in kind with lips and tongue and hands that drove her back into the heaven she had visited before, this time knowing it would be shared always and for ever, with him.

He folded his arms around her waist as they gazed into the neglected refrigerator.

'I'm hungry,' she sighed as she tried to ignore his roving hands.

'Me too. Come back to bed.'

She laughed and trickled her fingers into his hair. 'You've an evening surgery at five.'

'That gives us an hour. Bob's on till then.'

'Perfect planning.' She eyed him suspiciously. 'You and your father both. He knew about everything that was happening at the surgery, didn't he?'

He grimaced and sat her down carefully at the table, producing the lonely bottle of wine which occupied the entire shelf of the fridge. 'He did indeed.'

'How?'

Pouring two glasses of wine, he handed her one. 'We had a mole in our midst. This mole secretly made hospital visits, spilling the beans for reasons best known to devious little moles. Not that it mattered. Theo took it well, almost as a bit of a joke. I think Corinne's duplicity amused him.'

'Corinne?'

He took hold of her hands across the table, curling them into little fists within his own, his expression amused. 'I suppose I should thank her.'

'For going behind your back?'

'For making it easier in a strange kind of way. For the first time in my life, Theo accepted my help. It meant a lot to me. Then I realised I was feeling totally fulfilled in general practice. And when I thought about it, really thought about it, I knew I couldn't go back to being the person I was.'

She swallowed. 'You're sure? In six months' time you won't feel differently?'

He squeezed her hands. 'What do I have to say to convince you?'

She smiled. 'Just keep telling me you love me.'

'Daisy, it frightens me to think I could have lost you. Life seemed unbearable when I considered going back to Florida, to the person I had been before I met you. I love you, Daisy, and I always will.'

Tears smarted in her eyes. 'Oh, Josh. I really did think you were a confirmed bachelor. I thought...'

'I was, my darling,' he said quietly, 'until I met you. You've changed my life; you're so very special to me.' He grinned softly. 'And once I'd decided there was no way you were going to escape me I simply rescheduled this morning's appointments for tonight, asked Bob to swap Sunday with me for today and rang Emily, who said she was ready to come back.'

She sighed dazedly. 'But what about Corinne?'

He glanced at his watch, pulling up the sleeve of his towelling robe. 'On her way to the States as we speak.'

'Josh ... you can't be serious?'

He pulled a face. 'Deadly. She expressed a desire to work abroad and I provided her with contacts and telephone numbers. A friend agreed to put her up until she's found a job. The least I could do under the circumstances.'

Daisy stared incredulously at the bland expression on the face in front of her.

He laughed in self-derision. 'I knew Corinne was a mistake from the start, but I tried hedging my bets ... and lost. Miserably.'

He tugged her from her chair and into his arms, easing the thin straps of her camisole from her shoulders, bending down to brush his lips against her naked skin. 'I wish you hadn't started to dress. Come back to bed.'

'You'll be late...'

'No, I won't. I've got you as an alarm clock.'

'Don't bet on it.'

'You're beautiful,' he whispered as he drew the garment over her head and threaded out her arms, staring at the burgeoning freedom of her breasts and their tiny pink buds smiling up at him, beckoning him. 'You're beautiful, exciting, wonderful… I was so jealous. Jealous as hell,' he growled raggedly, lowering his head.

'Jealous of whom?' She cupped his head in her hands, staring into evasive grey eyes.

'Who do you think?'

She began to laugh. 'Peter? Oh, that's ridiculous!'

'Is it? I thought it was ridiculous too when the same little mole rang me one evening, just after the love of my life had deserted me for a fabled photo shoot, to say you had been spotted the day of the carnival cavorting in the Skylark with a tall, handsome man.'

Daisy's face turned scarlet.

'Somewhere near the truth, I see.'

She gulped. 'Was it … Corinne? What did she see?'

'Enough.'

'Josh, I–'

'Secrets already?' He shook his head and she couldn't be sure if he was angry, those grey eyes staring down at her with naked reproach.

'Was that why you came looking for me?'

He grimaced at her, pulling her towards him with a little shake. 'I was mad as hell. And I was jealous.'

She took a breath, whispering softly, 'There was no need, my darling, no need at all.'

He groaned, a sound which seemed to come from deep within him. 'Then prove I have nothing to be jealous of.'

She thrilled at his command, at her throbbing, needful body as she curved a hand around his cheek, dragging him forward, sliding herself against him, lost in the compelling glow of reawakened urges and sweet anticipation. 'I'll give you all the proof you will ever want,' she whispered caressingly, slipping her fingers behind her back as she kissed him...

To unplug the phone.

Just in case.

The publishers hope that this book has given you enjoyable reading. Large Print Books are especially designed to be as easy to see and hold as possible. If you wish a complete list of our books please ask at your local library or write directly to:

Dales Large Print Books
Magna House, Long Preston,
Skipton, North Yorkshire.
BD23 4ND

This Large Print Book, for people
who cannot read normal print,
is published under the auspices of

THE ULVERSCROFT FOUNDATION

... we hope you have enjoyed this book.
Please think for a moment about those
who have worse eyesight than you ...
and are unable to even read or enjoy
Large Print without great difficulty.

You can help them by sending a
donation, large or small, to:

**The Ulverscroft Foundation,
1, The Green, Bradgate Road,
Anstey, Leicestershire, LE7 7FU,
England.**
or request a copy of our brochure for
more details.

The Foundation will use all donations
to assist those people who are visually
impaired and need special attention
with medical research, diagnosis
and treatment.

Thank you very much for your help.